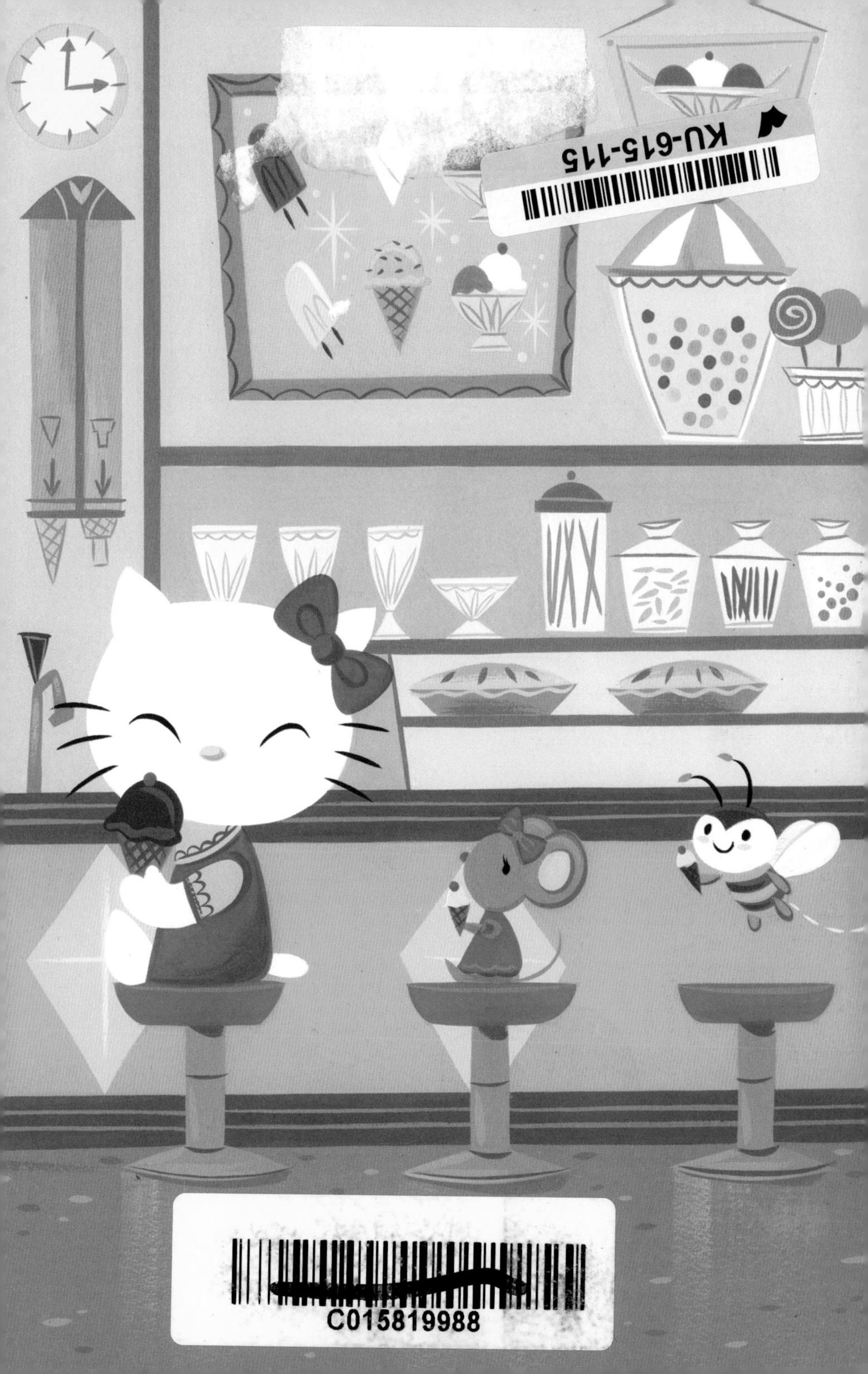

HELLO KITTY®
Delicious!

stories and art by
Jacob Chabot, Ian McGinty
and Jorge Monlongo

hello kitty shorts by
Stephanie Buscema

HELLO KITTY

Here We Go!

Stories and Art Jacob Chabot, Ian McGinty, Jorge Monlongo
Endpapers and Shorts Stephanie Buscema

Cover Art Jacob Chabot
Cover and Book Design Shawn Carrico
Editor Traci N. Todd

Printed in China

Published by VIZ Media, LLC
P.O. Box 77010
San Francisco, CA 94107

10 9 8 7 6 5 4 3 2 1
First printing, January 2014

"Hot Stuff," "Banana Split," "Berry Big Problem," and "Piece of Cake"
Stories and art by Jacob Chabot

"Martian Munchies"
Story and art by Jorge Monlongo

"Food Fright"
Story by Traci N. Todd, art by Ian McGinty, colors by Michael E. Wiggam

"Sweet Dreams"
Story and art by Ian McGinty, colors by Michael E. Wiggam

"Ice Cream," "Guess How Many," and "How to Bake a Cake"
Stories and art by Stephanie Buscema

RATED A FOR ALL AGES
PARENTAL ADVISORY
HELLO KITTY: DELICIOUS!
is rated A and is suitable for readers of all ages.
ratings.viz.com

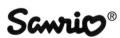

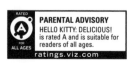

Contents

Family and Friends 6

Hot Stuff................................ 9

Ice Cream 15

Martian Munchies 16

Banana Split 22

Sweet Dreams 25

Guess How Many 34

Berry Big Problem................ 35

Food Fright........................... 45

Piece of Cake 55

How to Bake a Cake 61

Creators 62

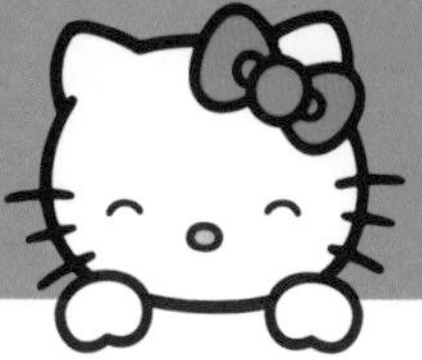

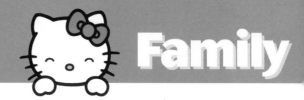

Family

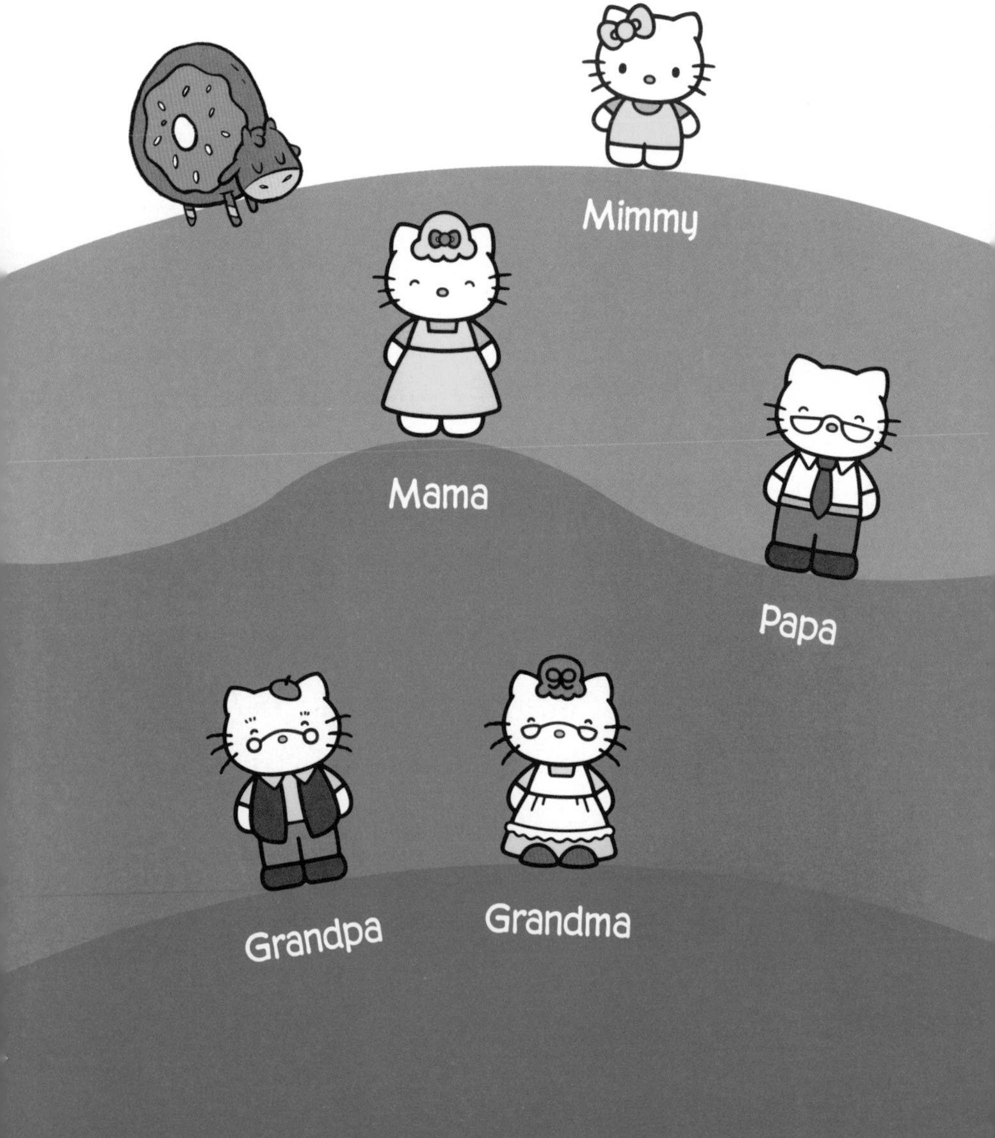
Mimmy
Mama
Papa
Grandpa
Grandma

and Friends

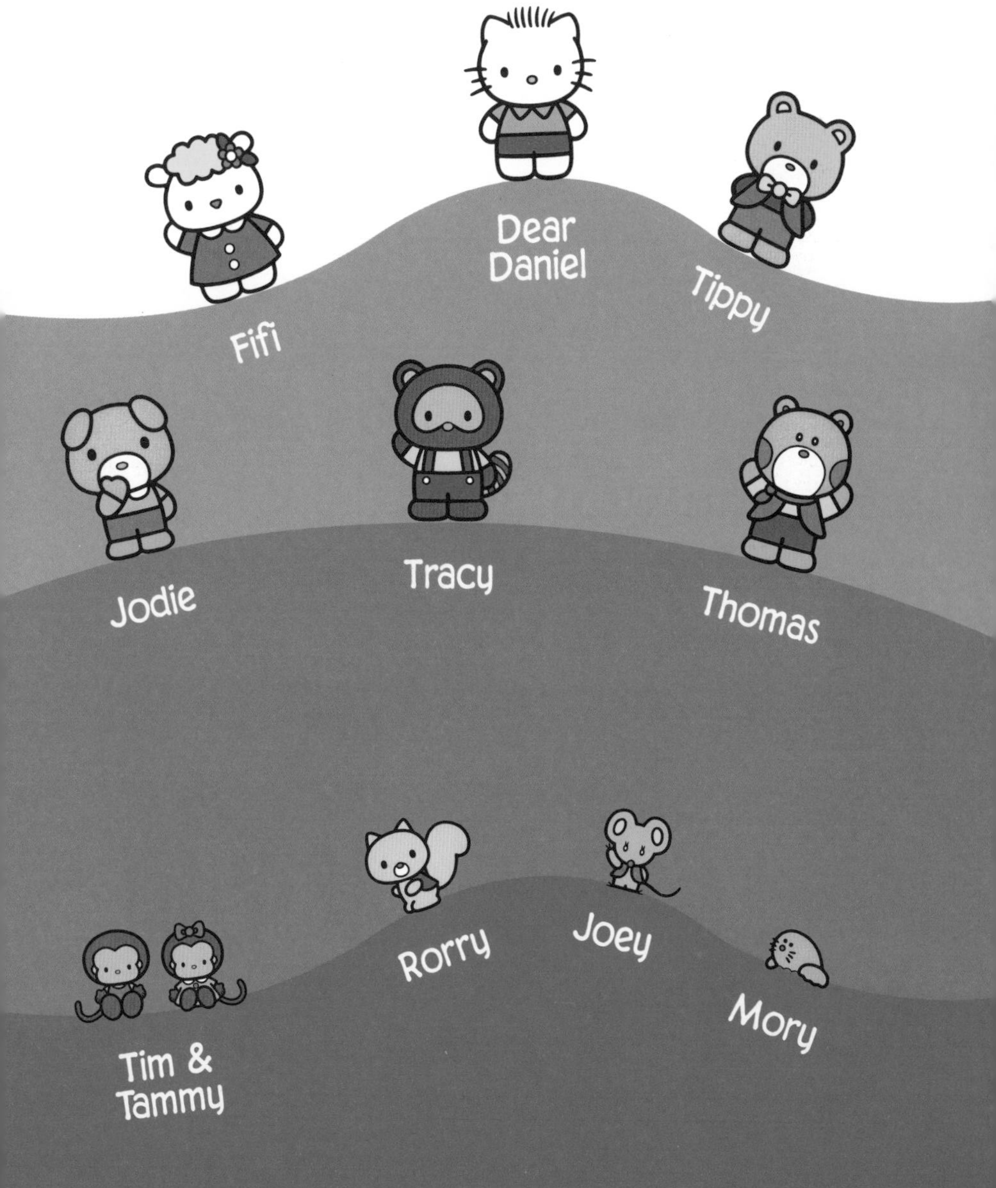
Dear
Daniel
Fifi
Tippy
Jodie
Tracy
Thomas
Rorry
Joey
Mory
Tim &
Tammy

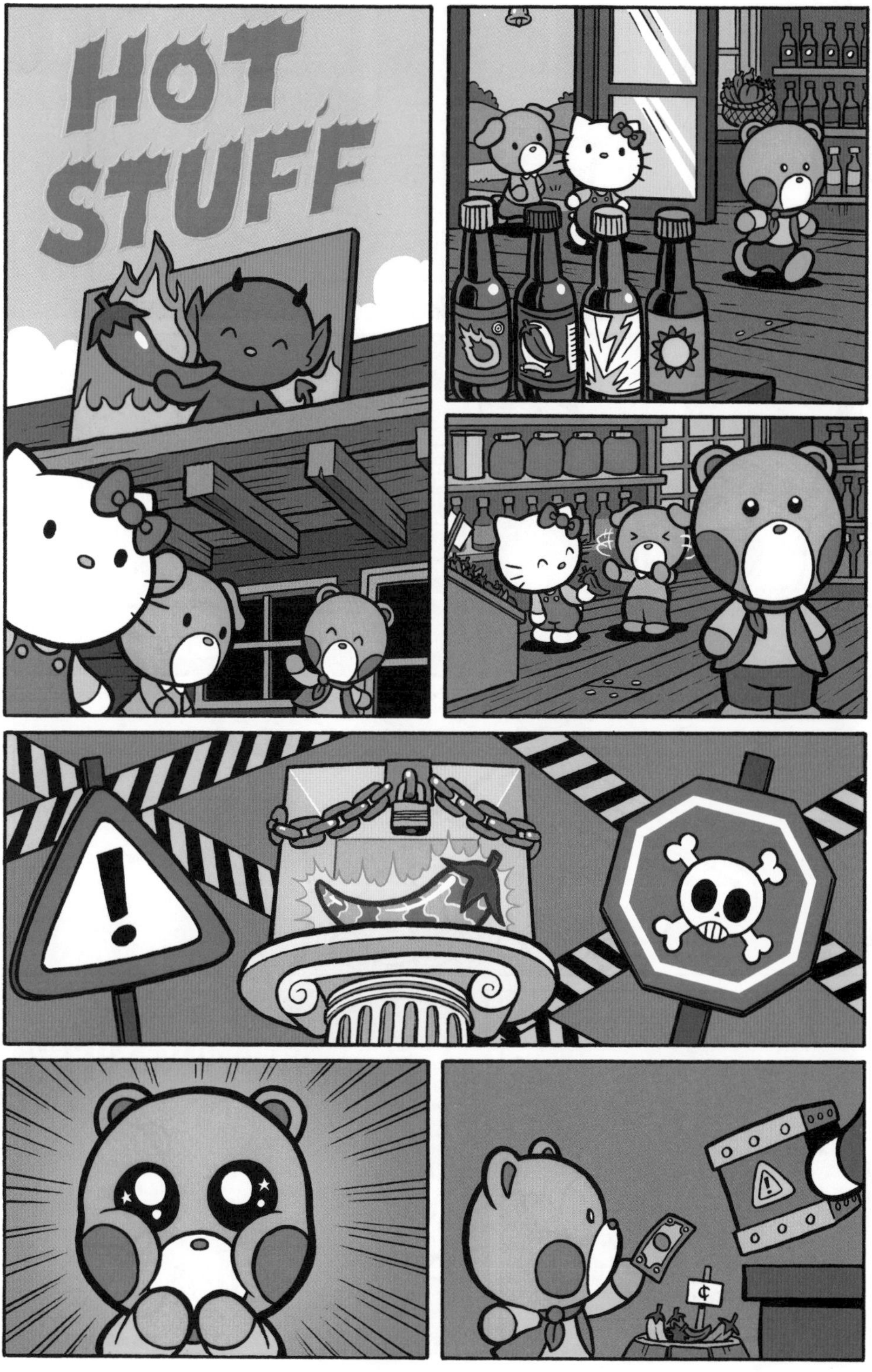
HOT STUFF

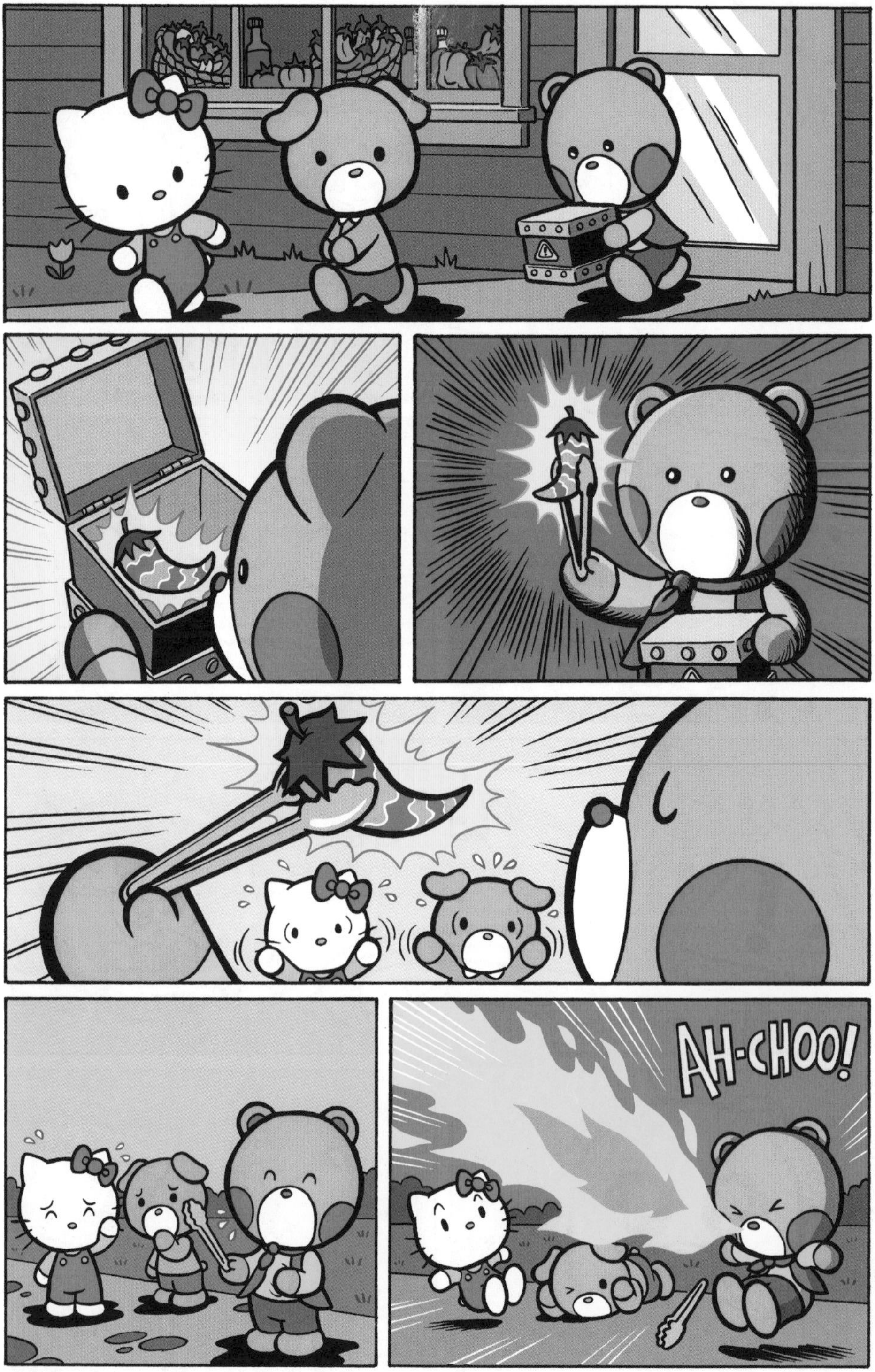
AH-CHOO!

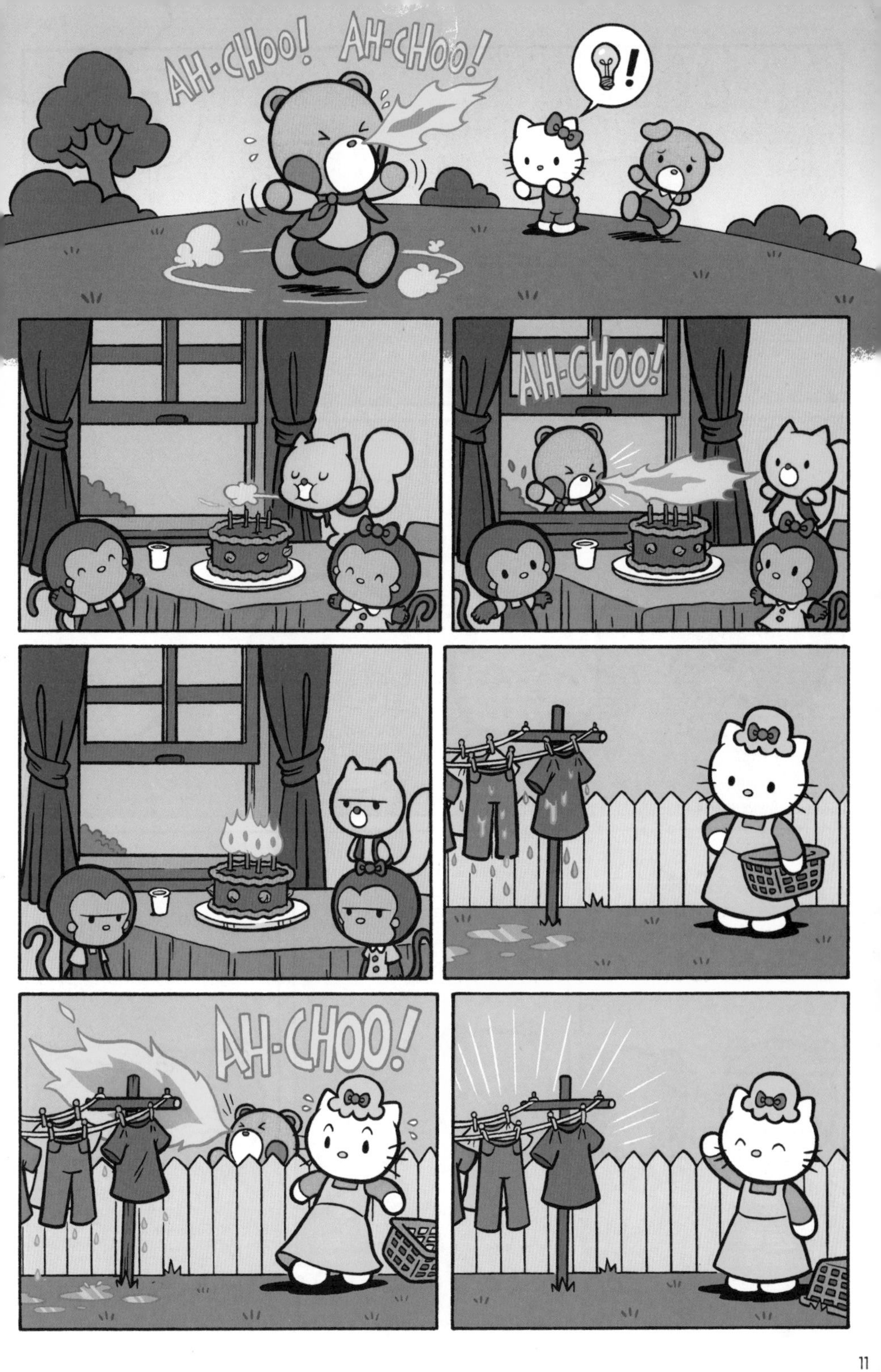
AH-CHOO! AH-CHOO!
!
AH-CHOO!
AH-CHOO!

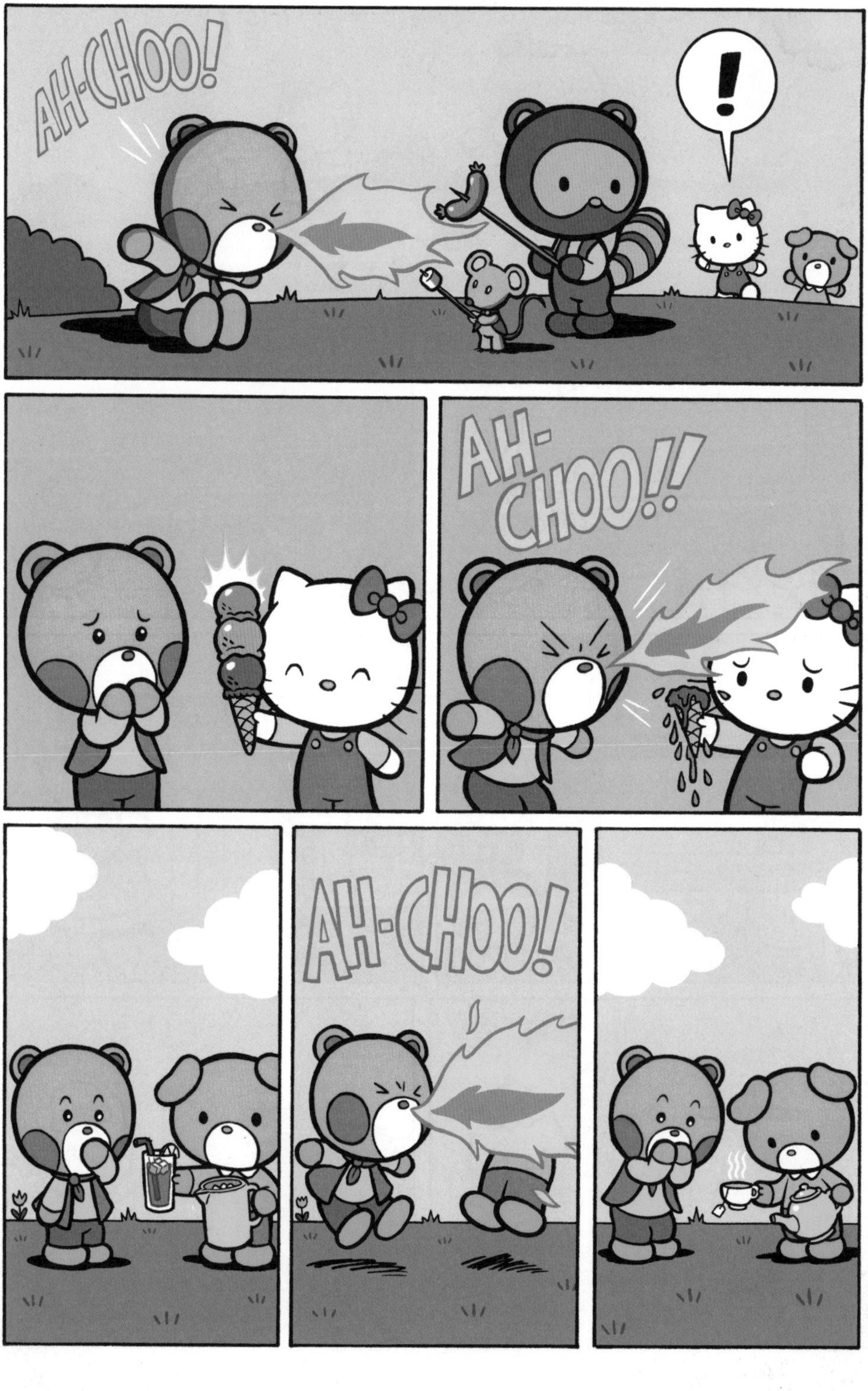
AH-CHOO!
!
AH-CHOO!!
AH-CHOO!

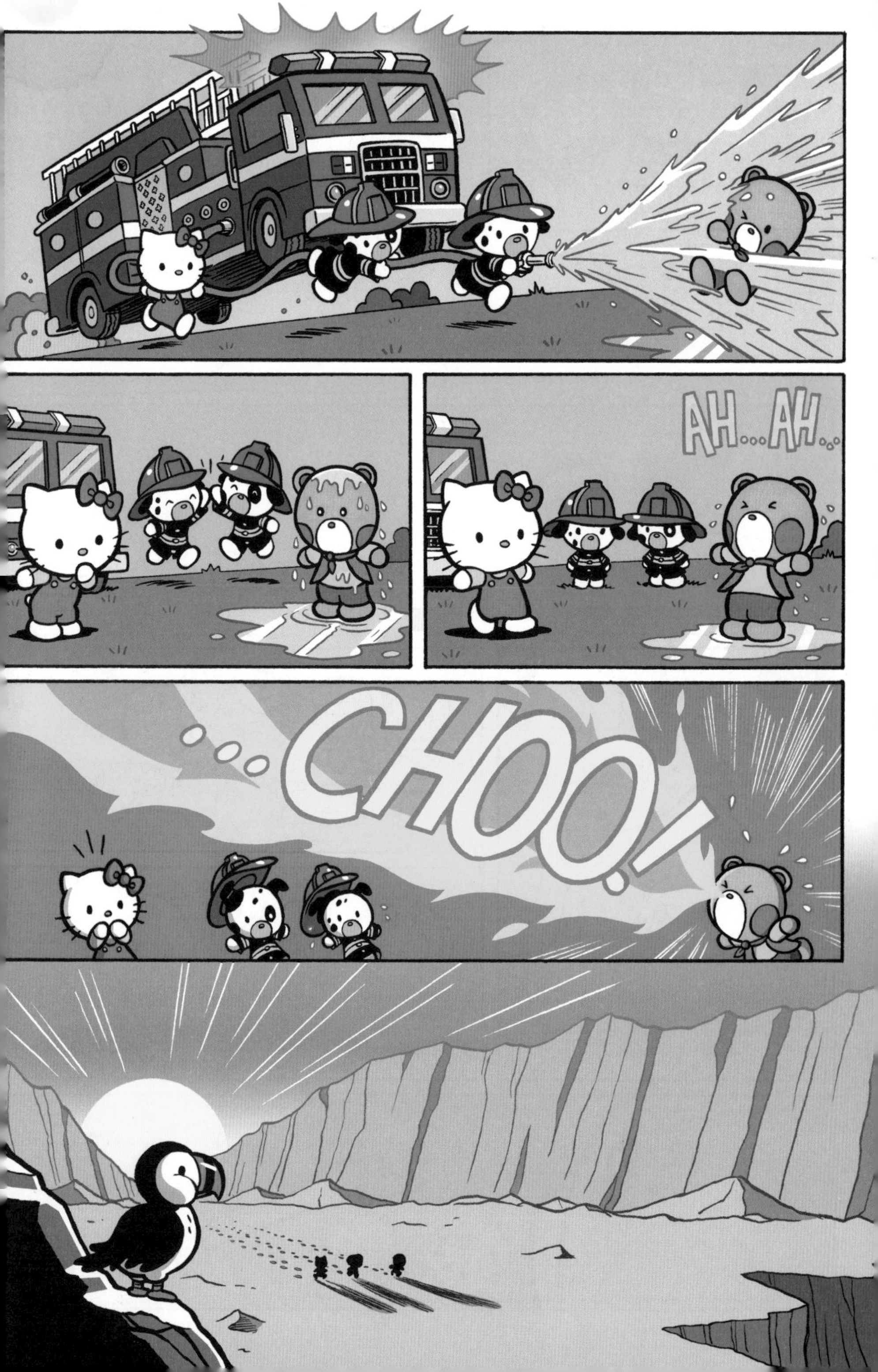
AH...AH...
...CHOO!

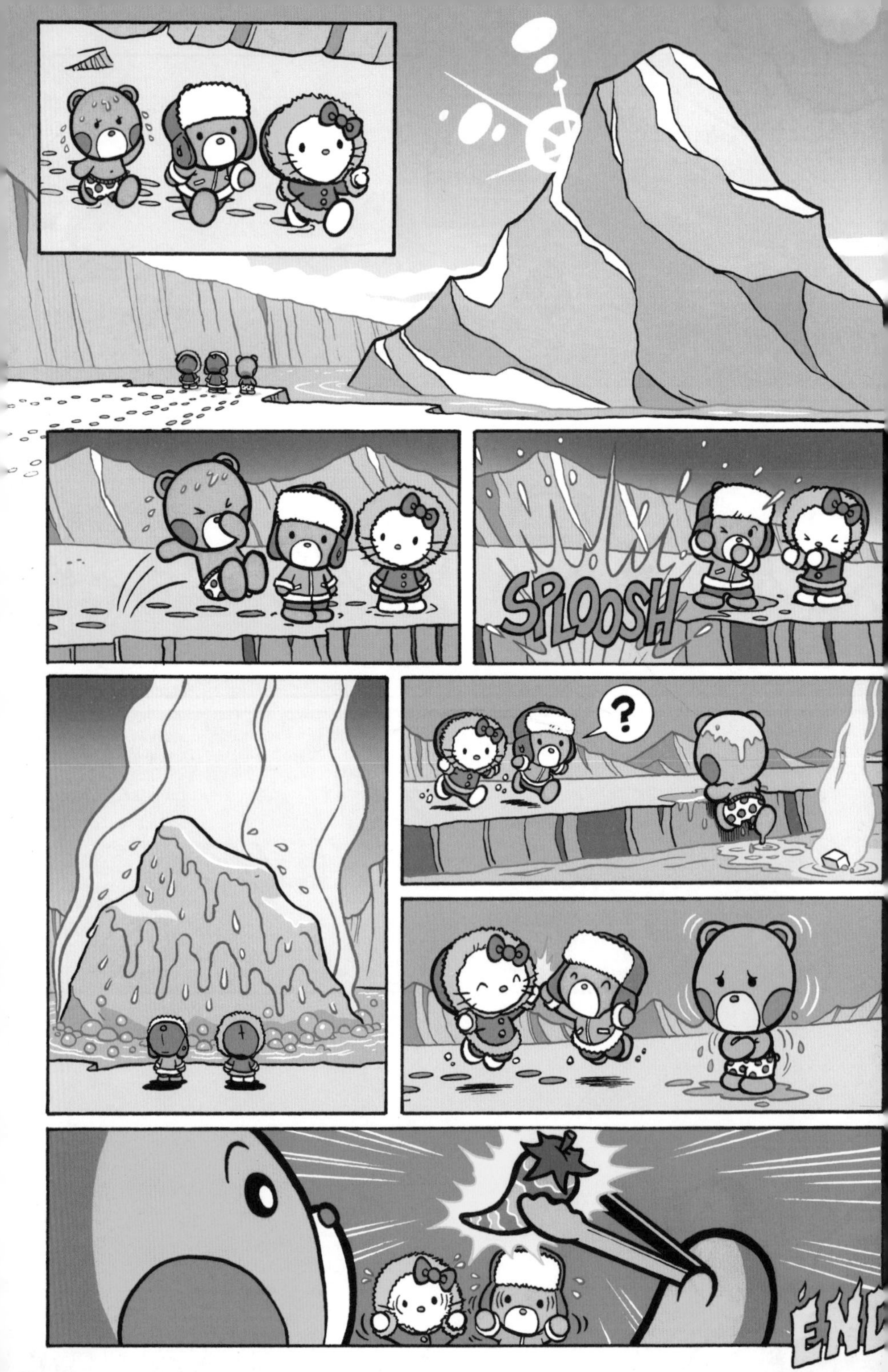
SPLOOSH
?
END

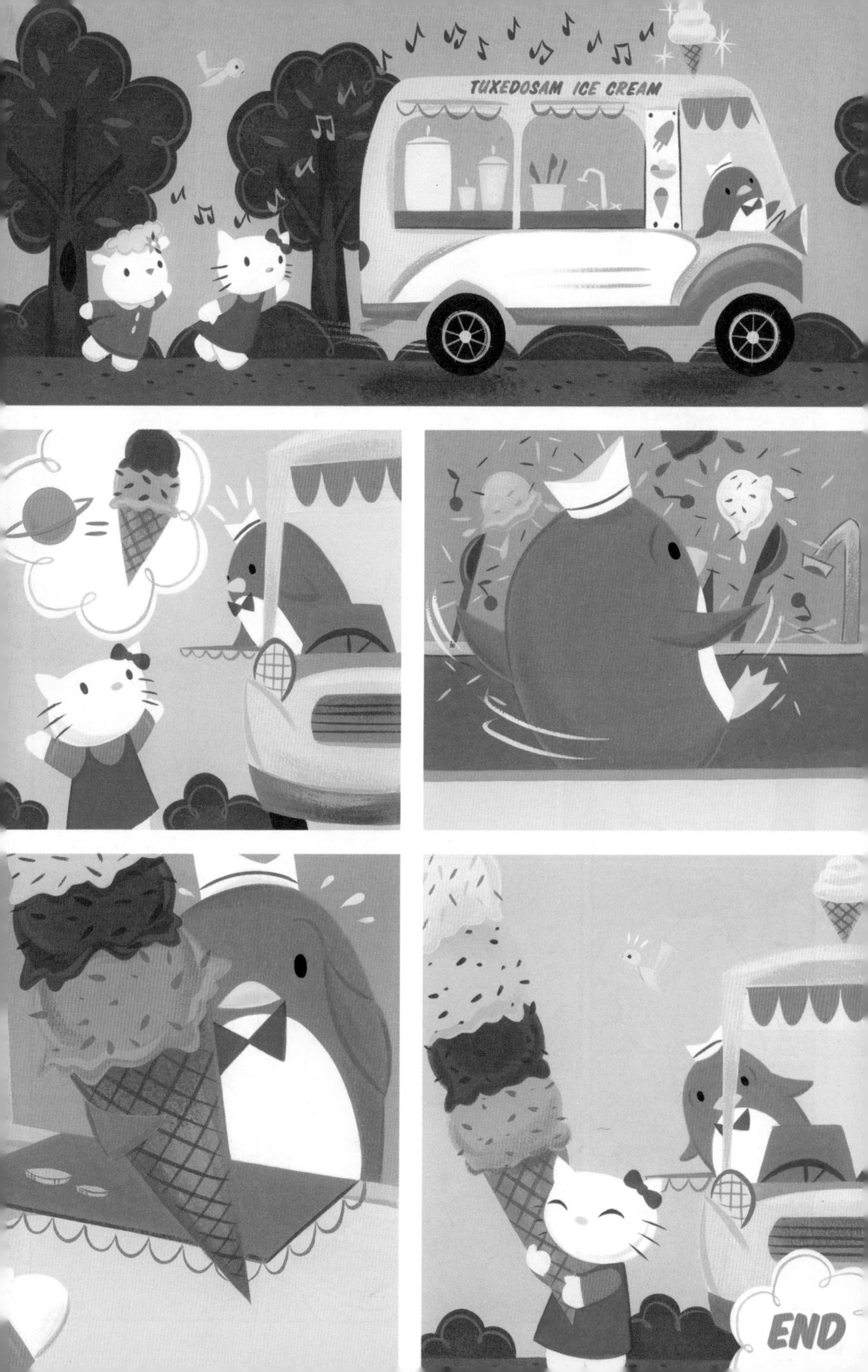
TUXEDOSAM ICE CREAM
END

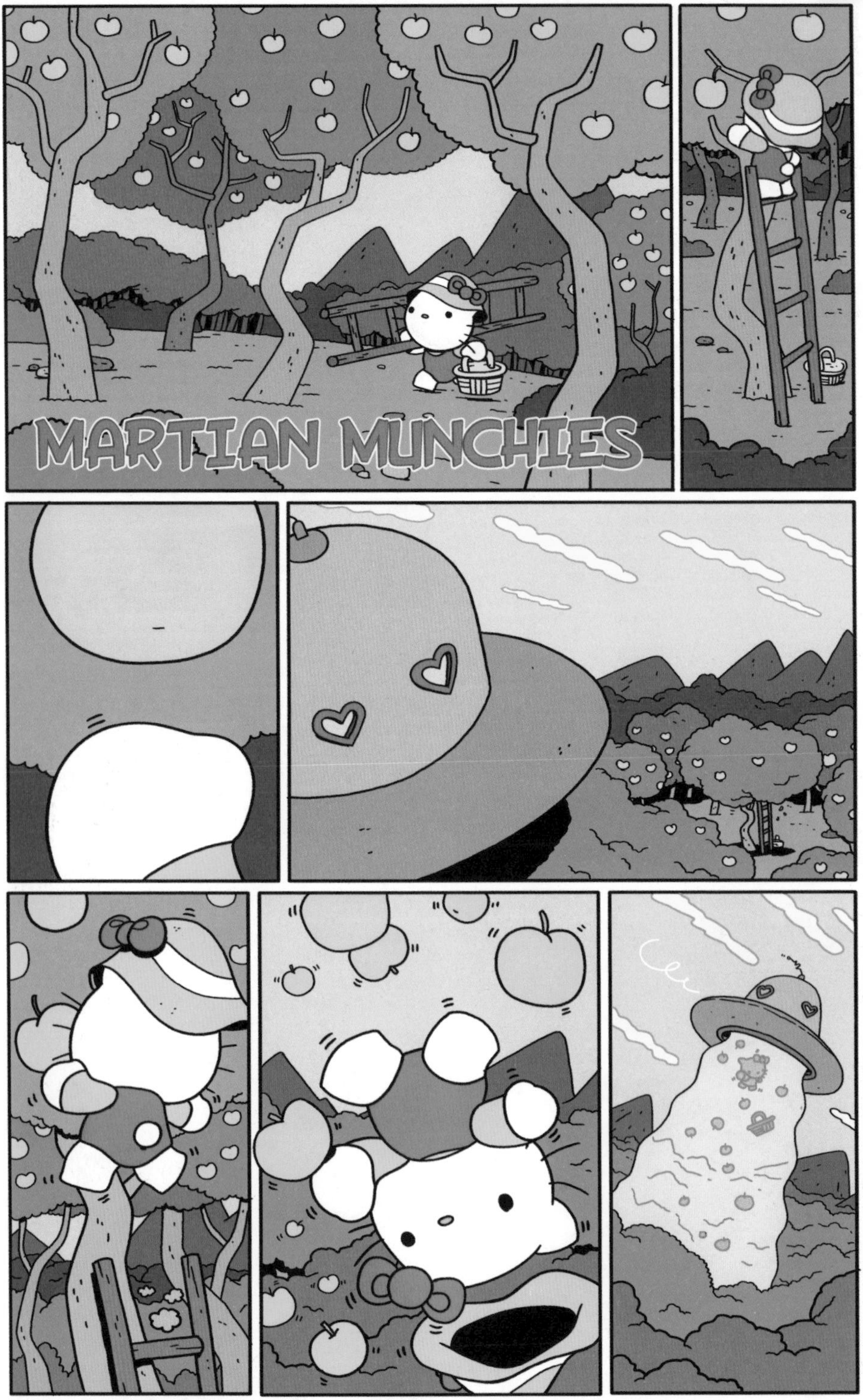
MARTIAN MUNCHIES

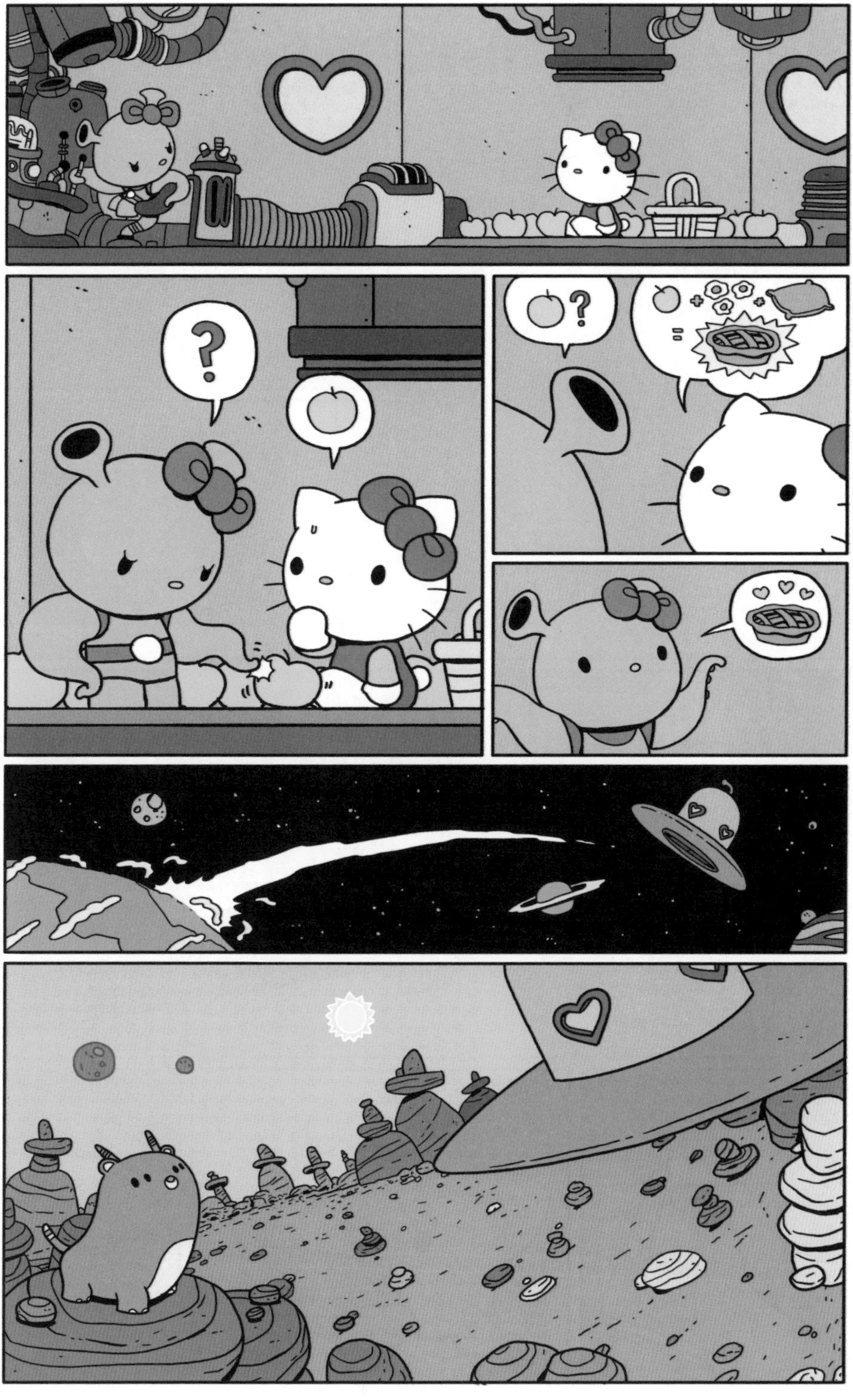
?
?
?

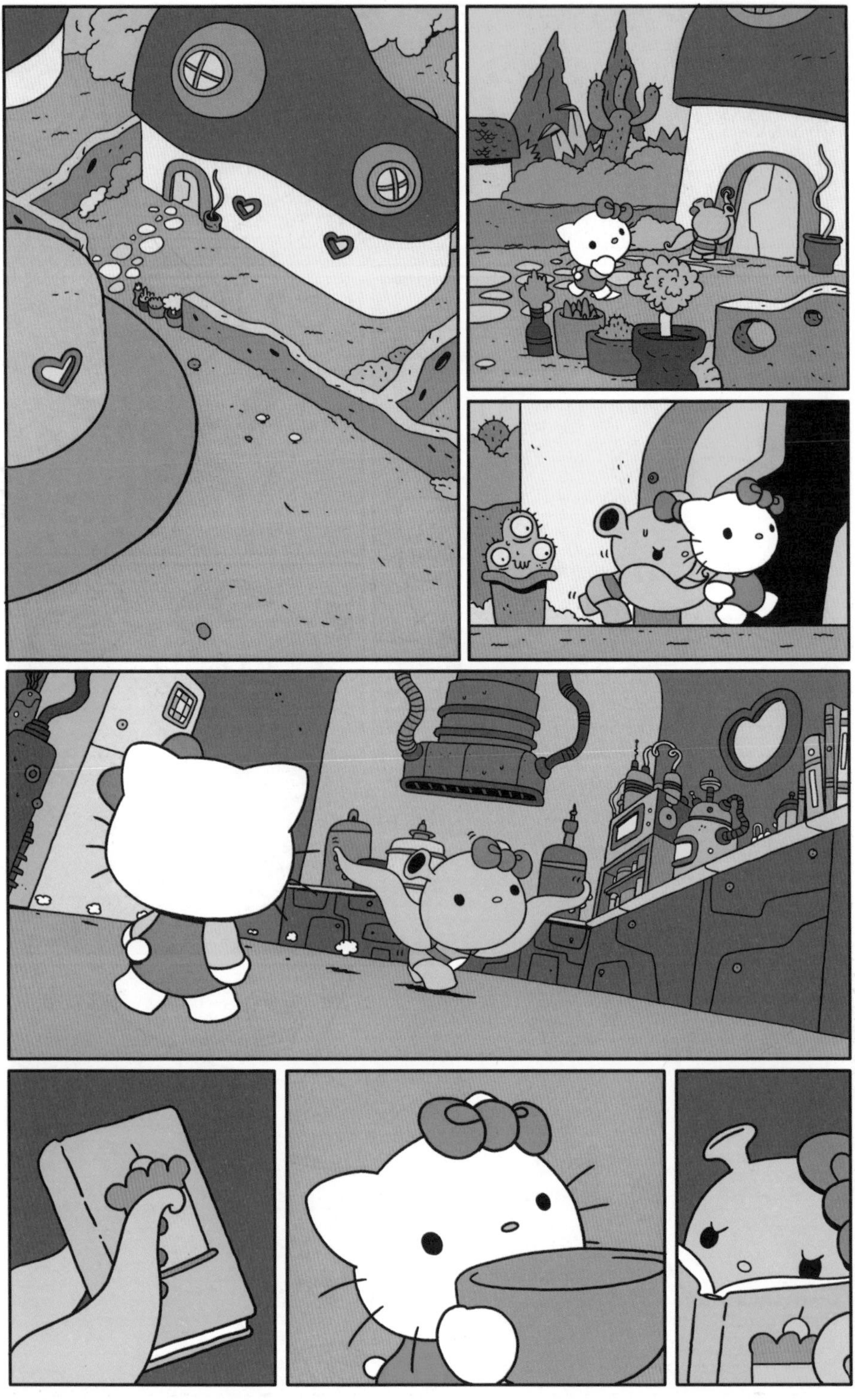

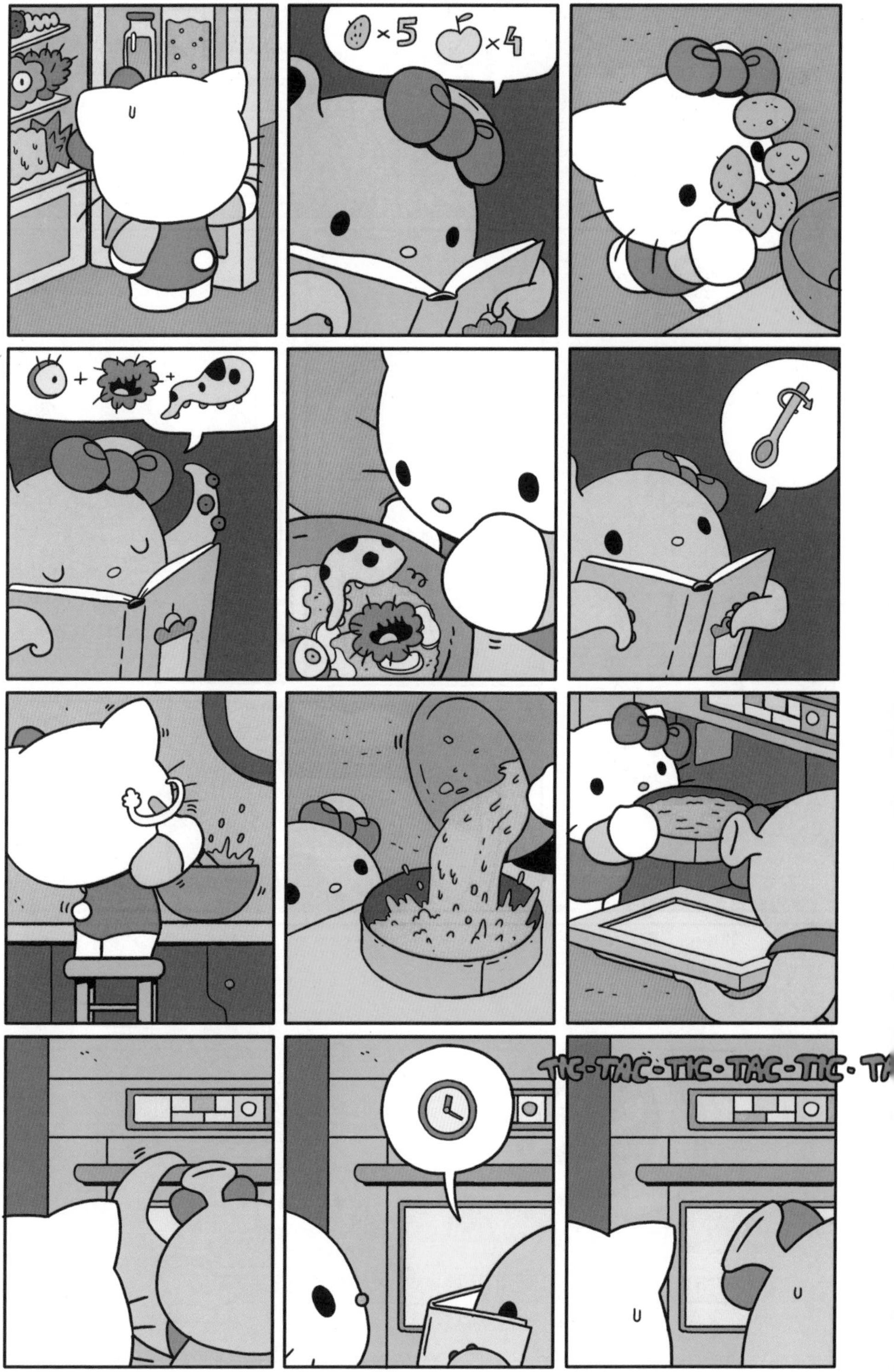
×5 ×4
TIC-TAC-TIC-TAC-TIC-TA

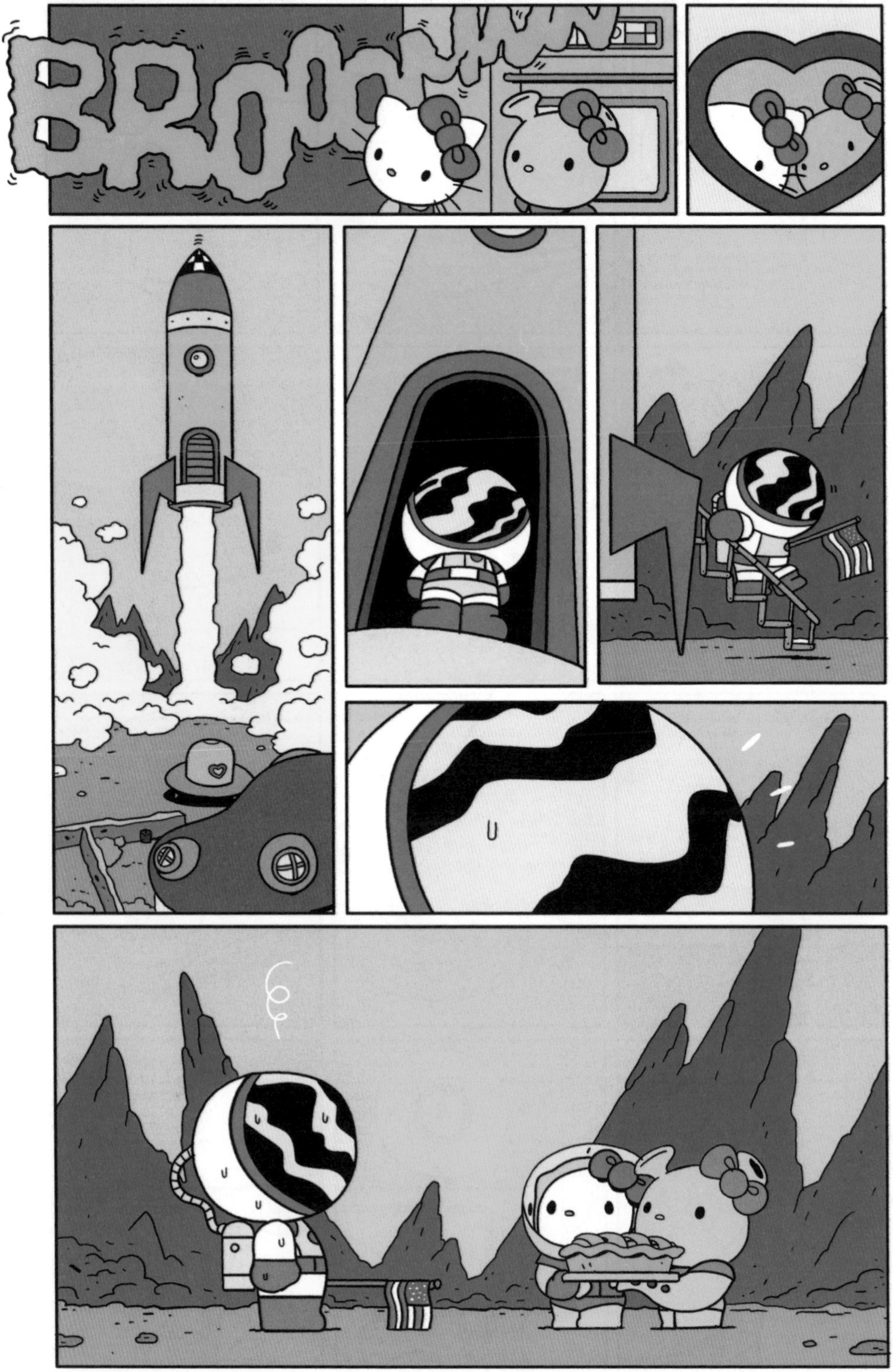
BROOOMM

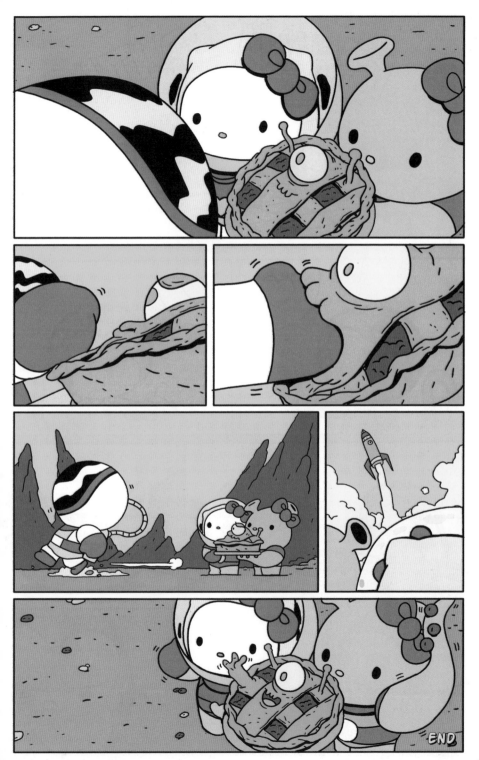

END

BANANA SPLIT!

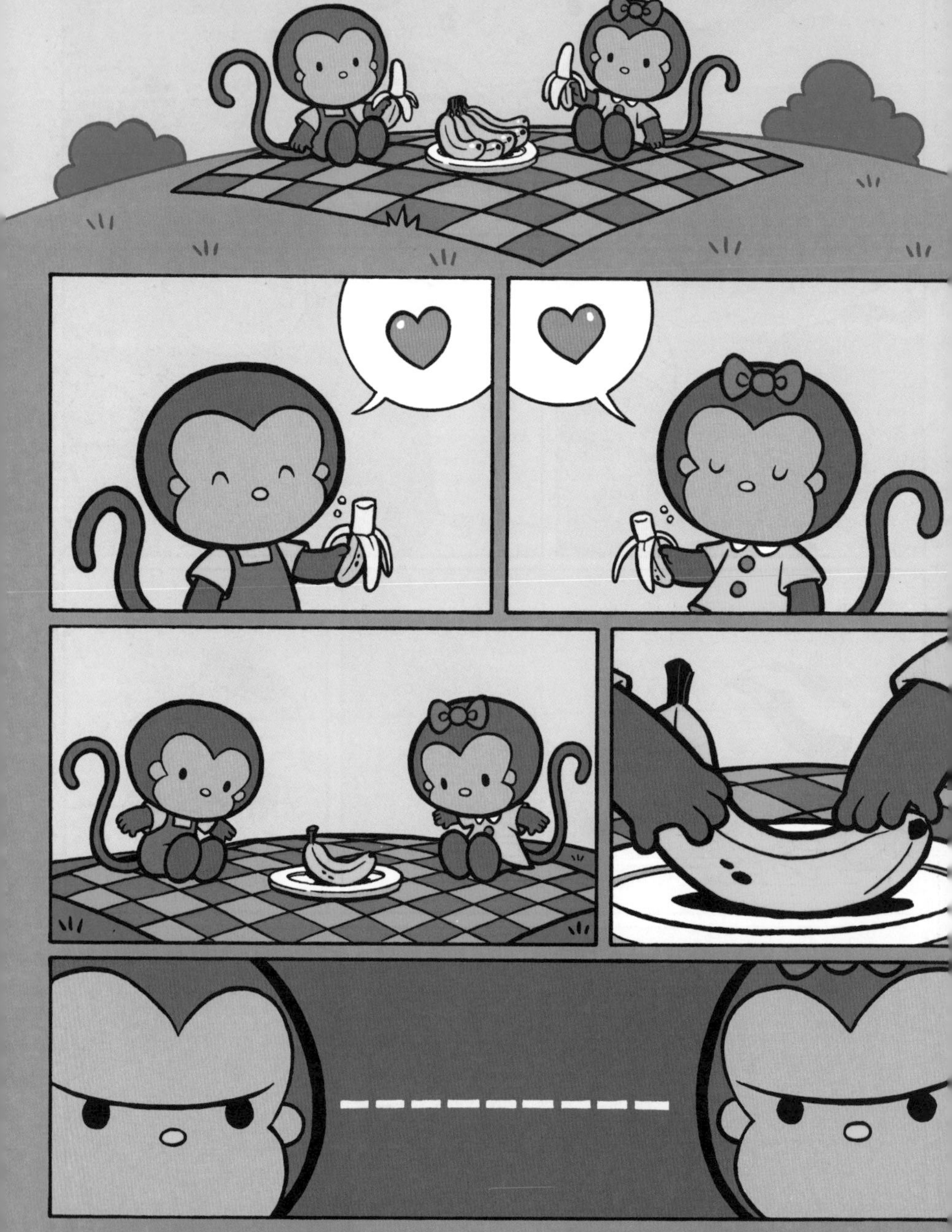

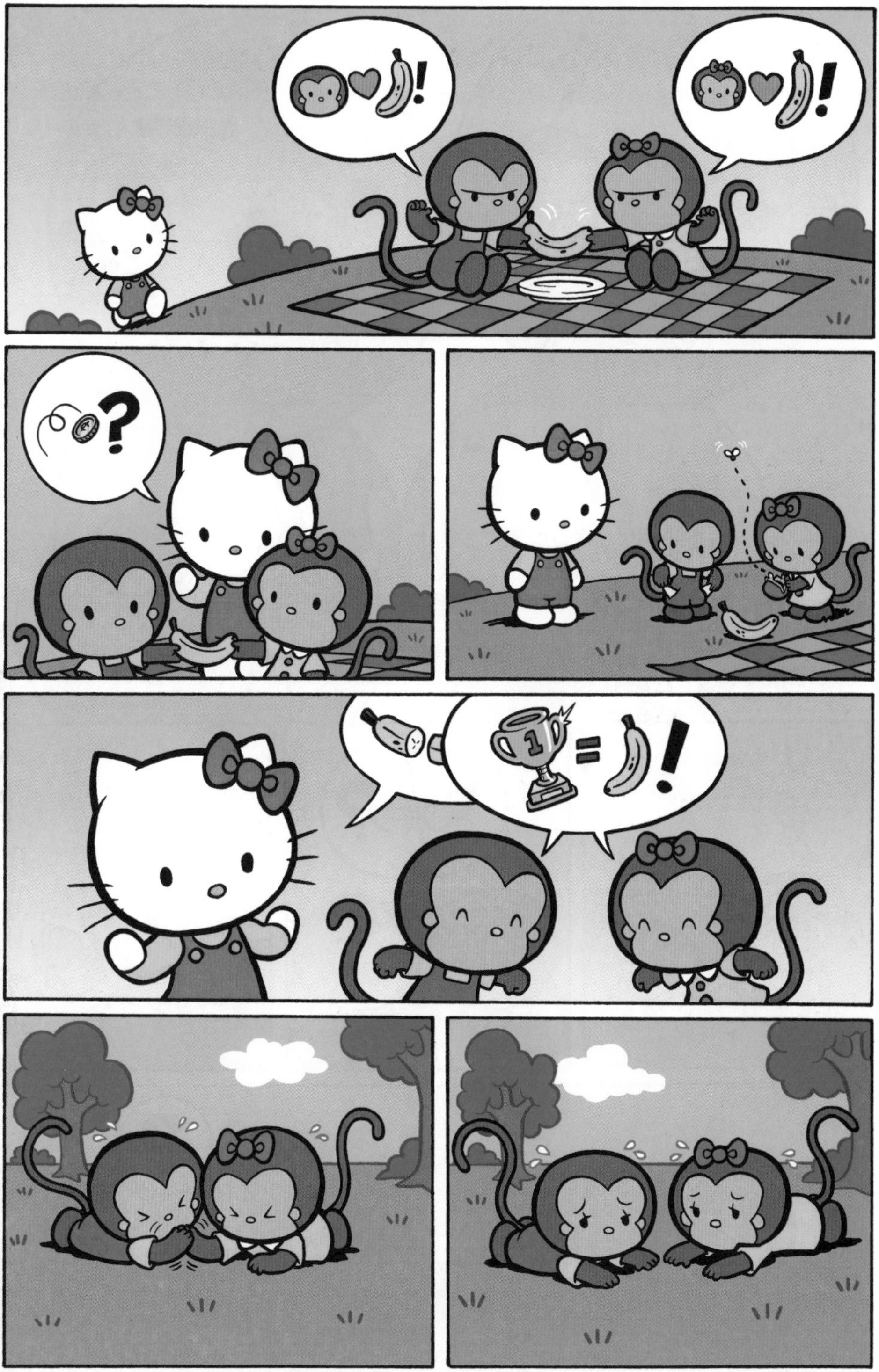

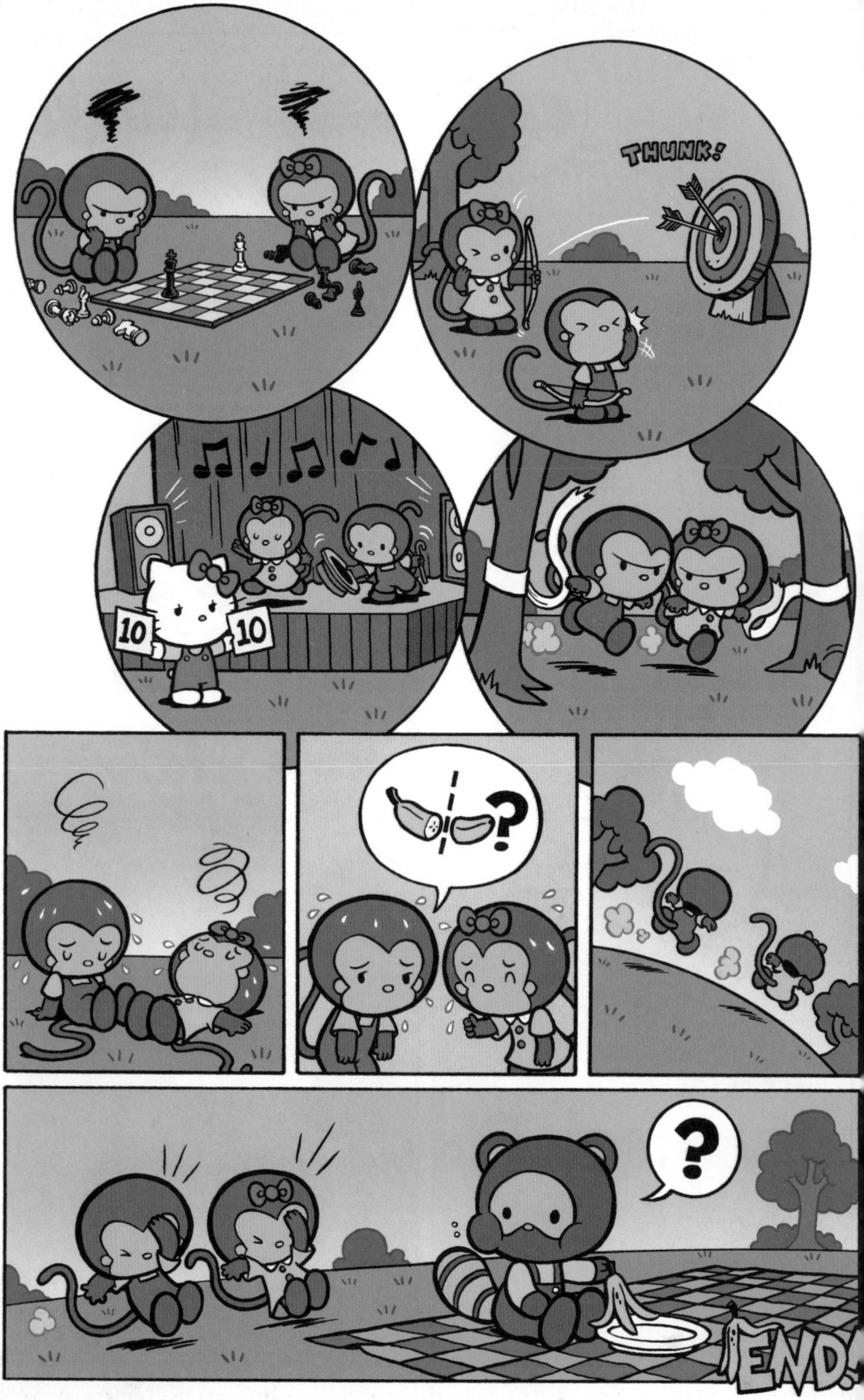
THUNK!
10
10
?
?
END

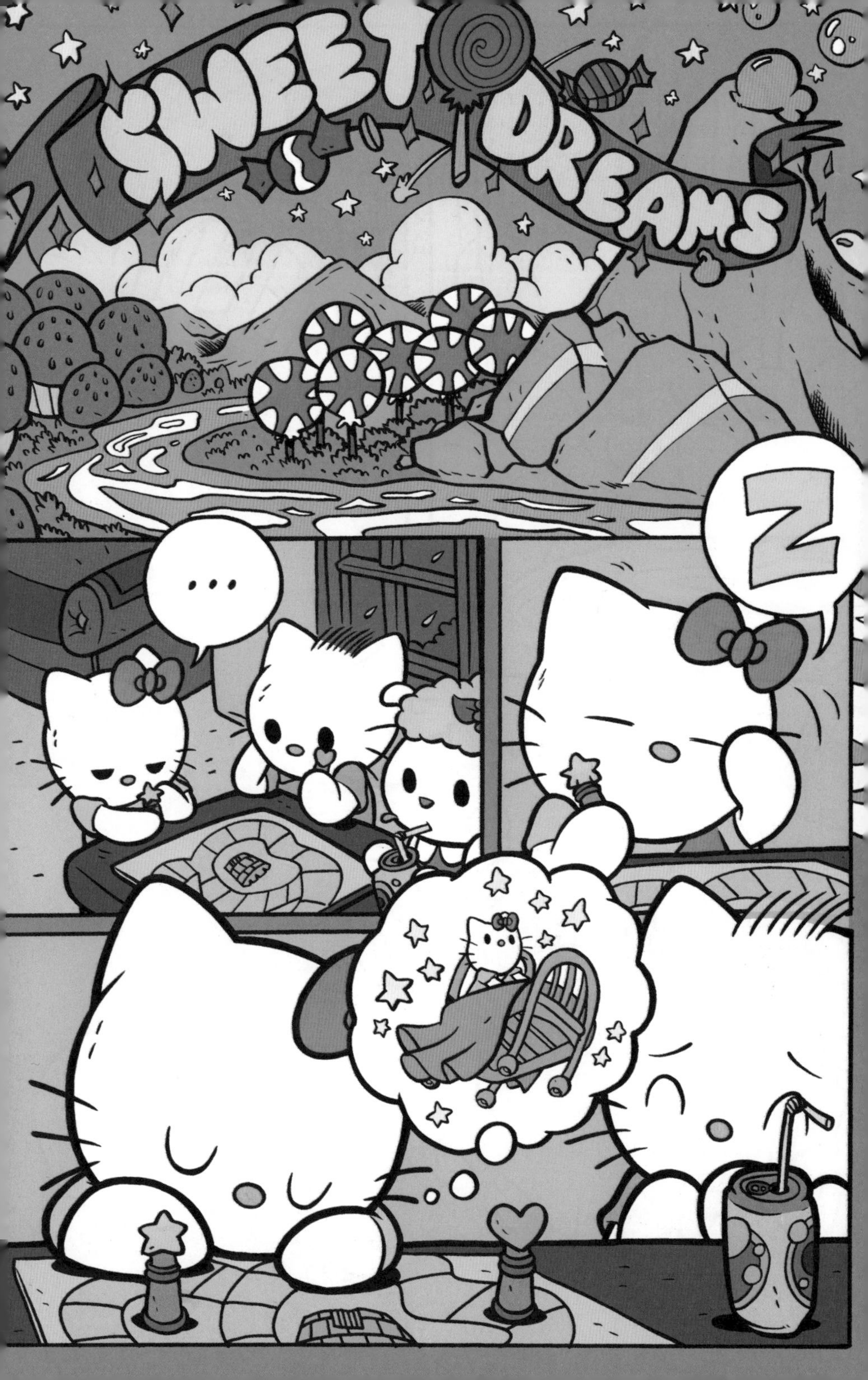
SWEET DREAMS
...
Z

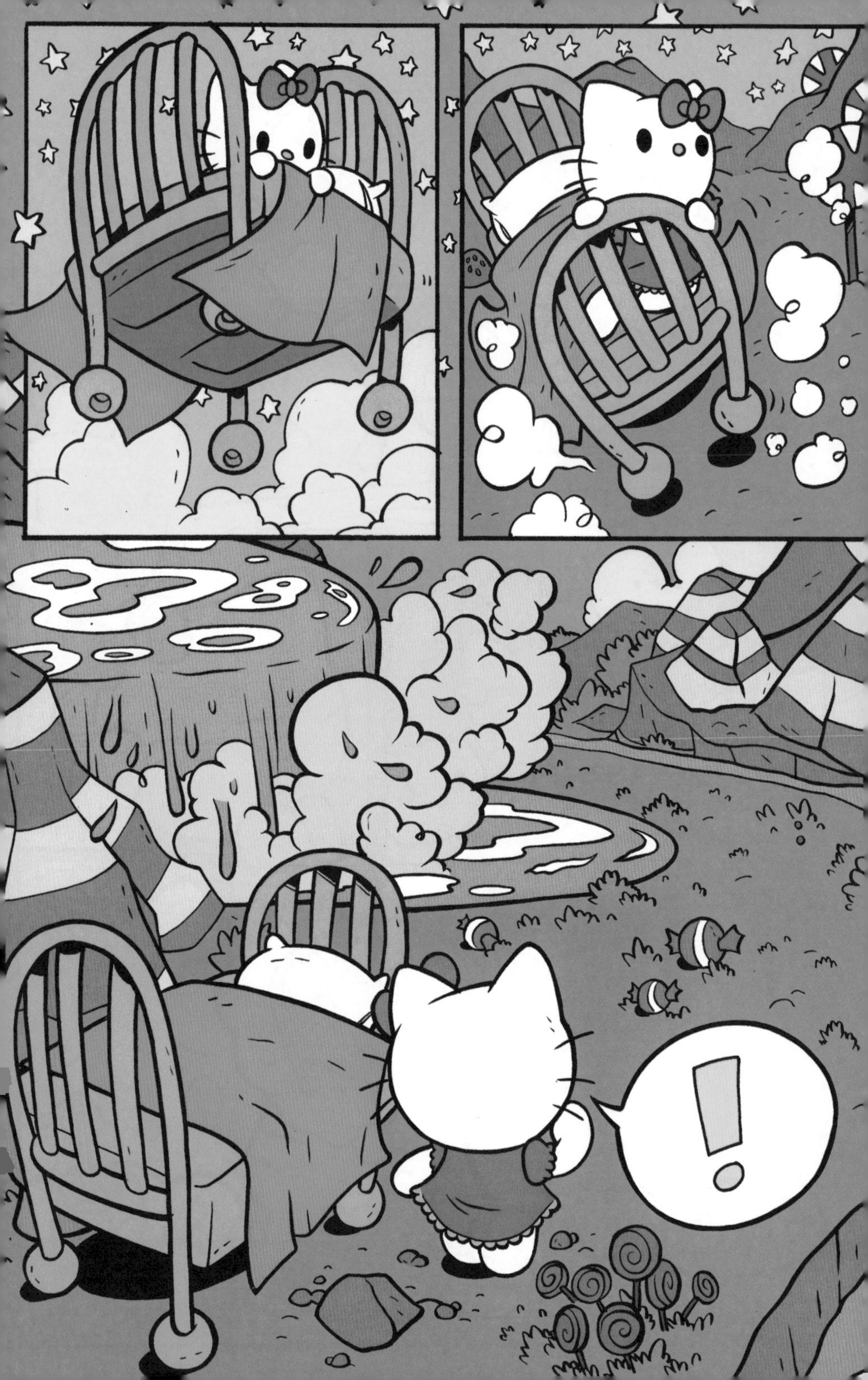
!

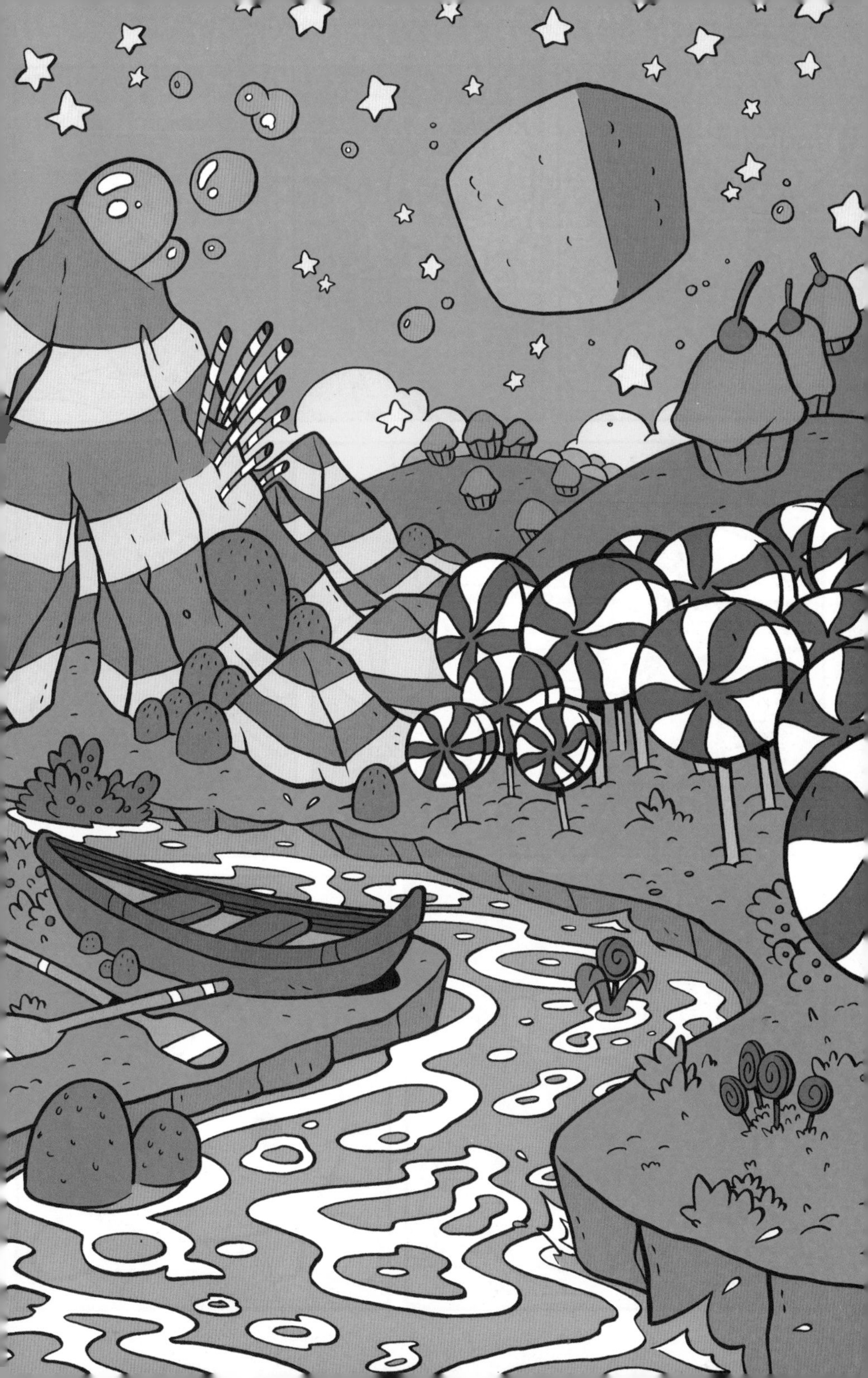

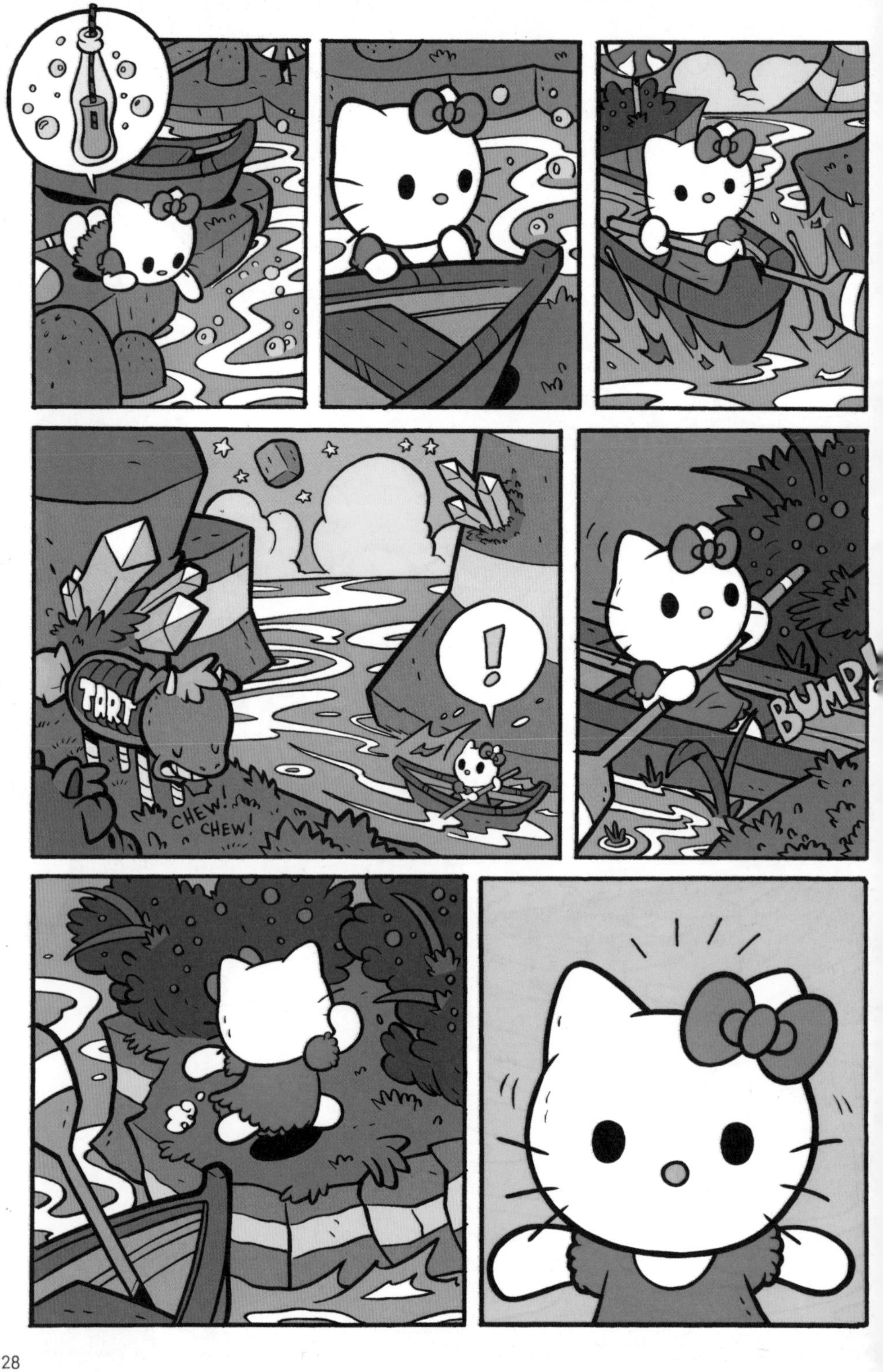
TART
!
CHEW!
CHEW!
BUMP!

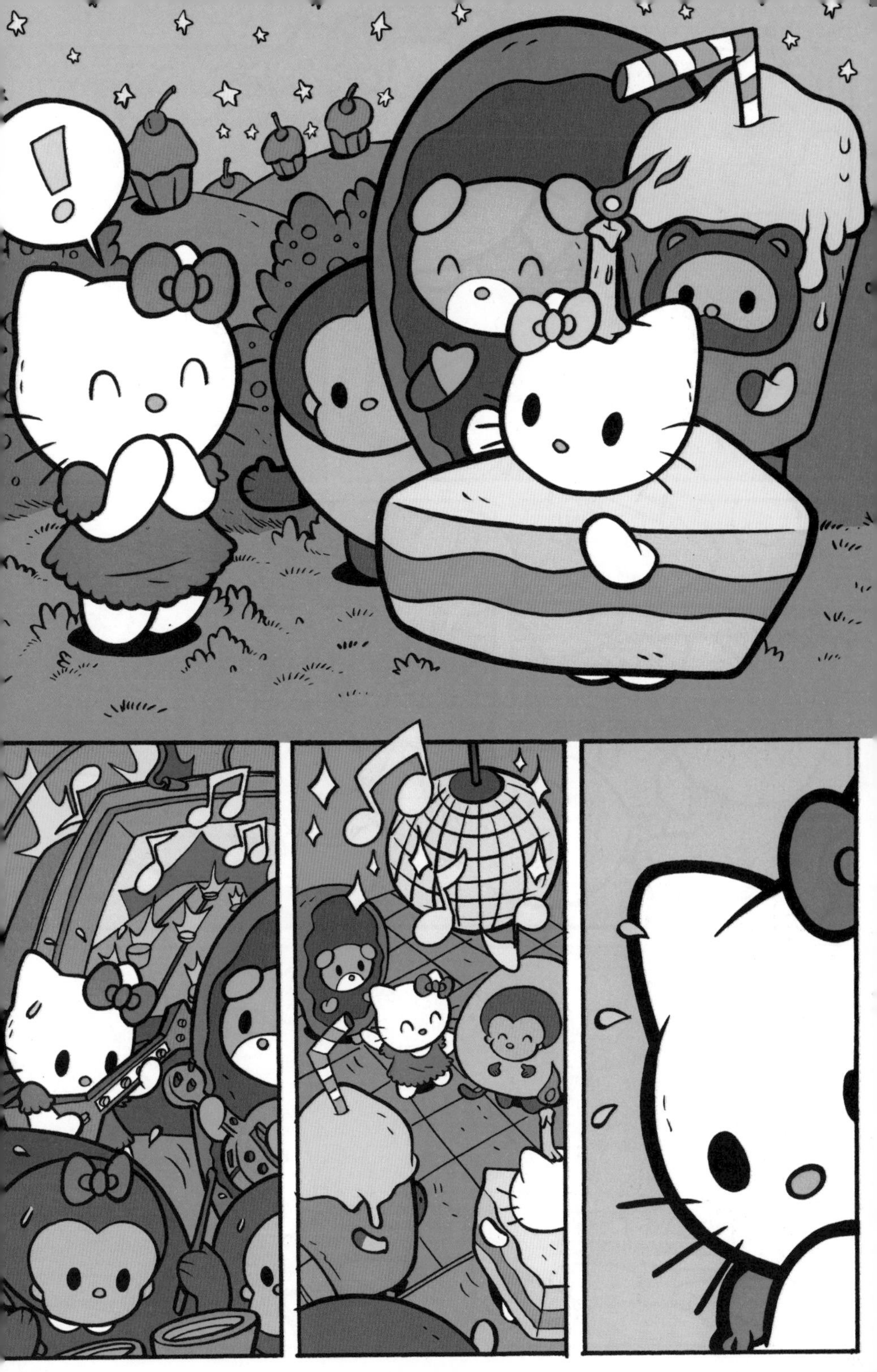
!

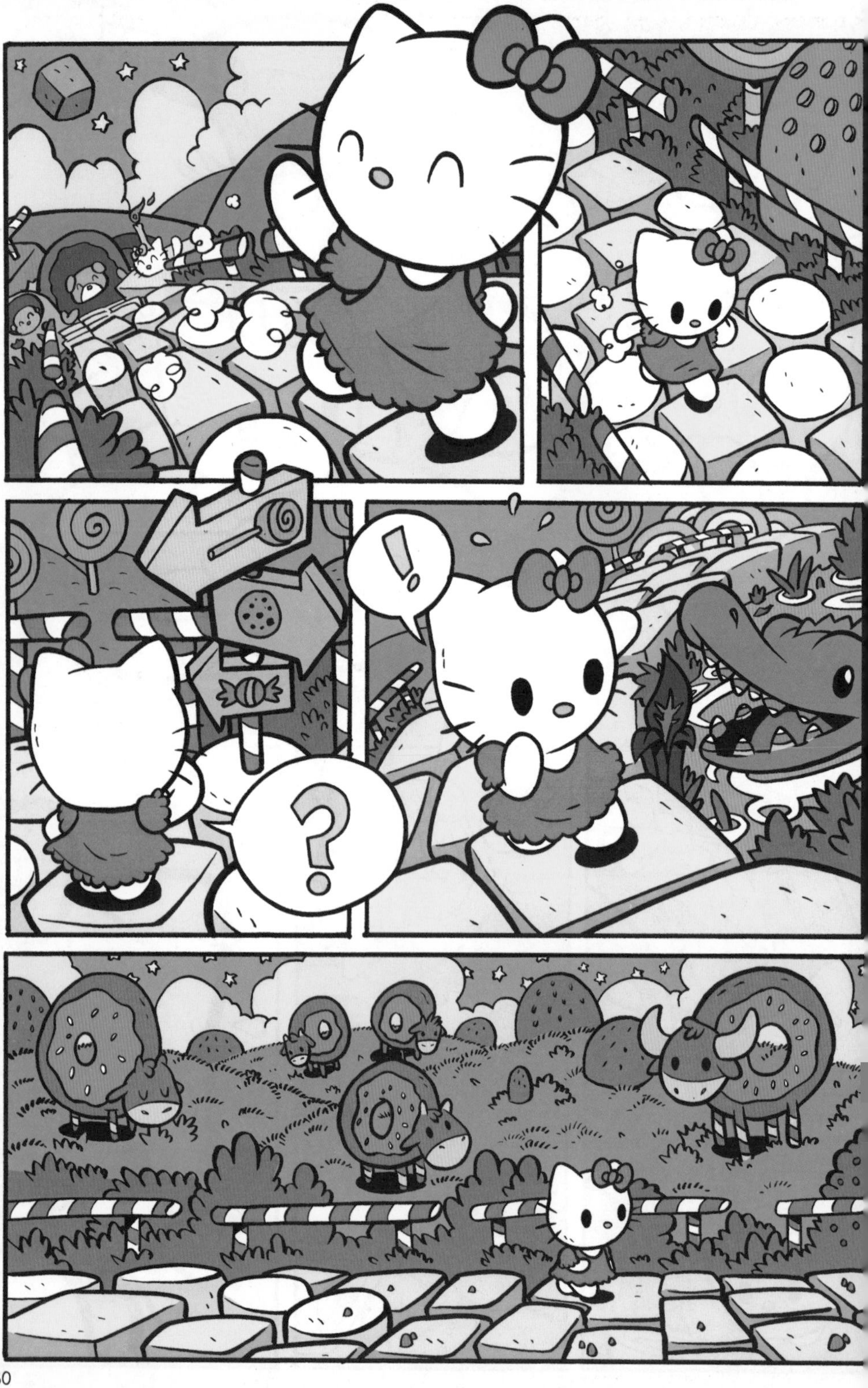
?
!

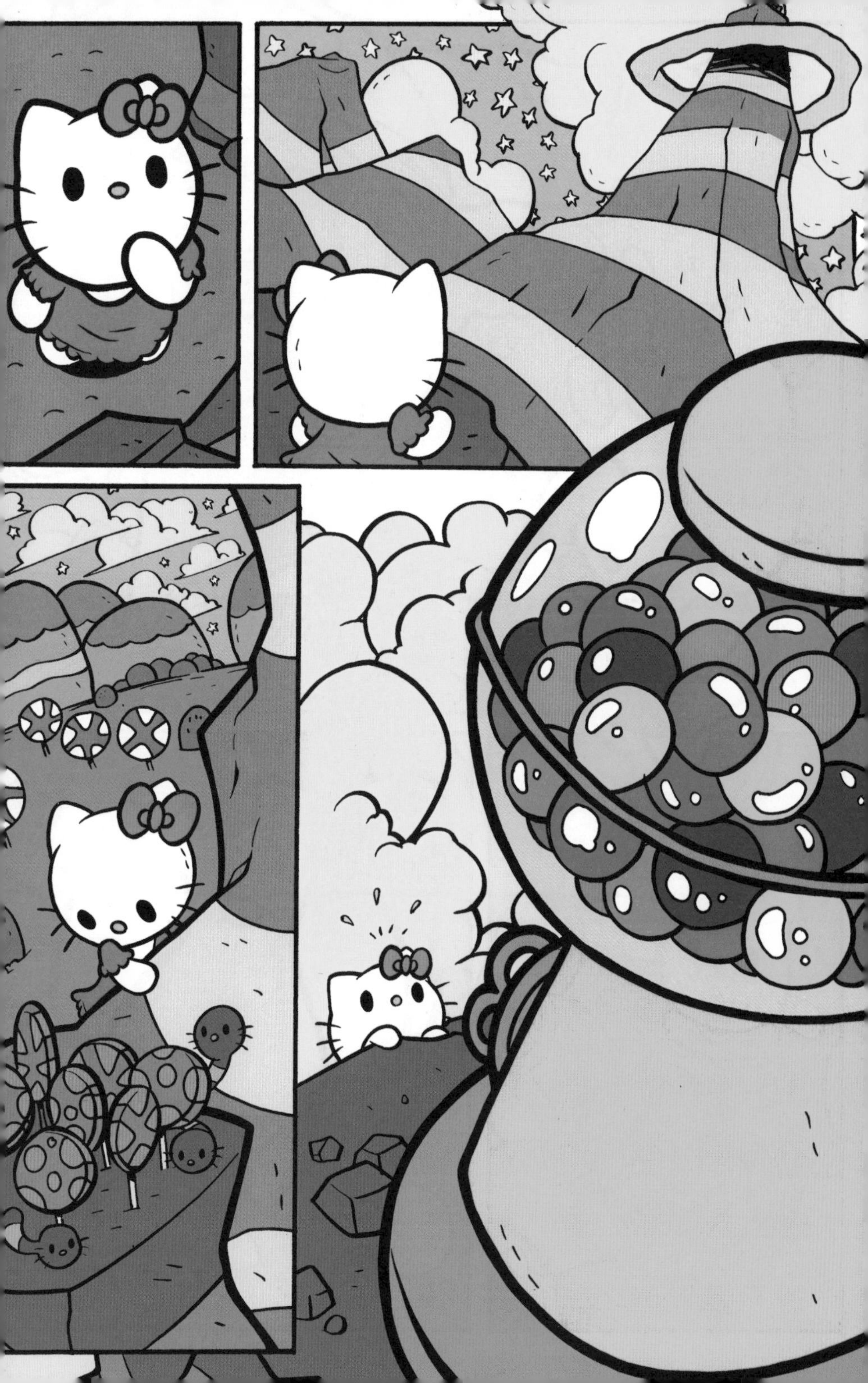

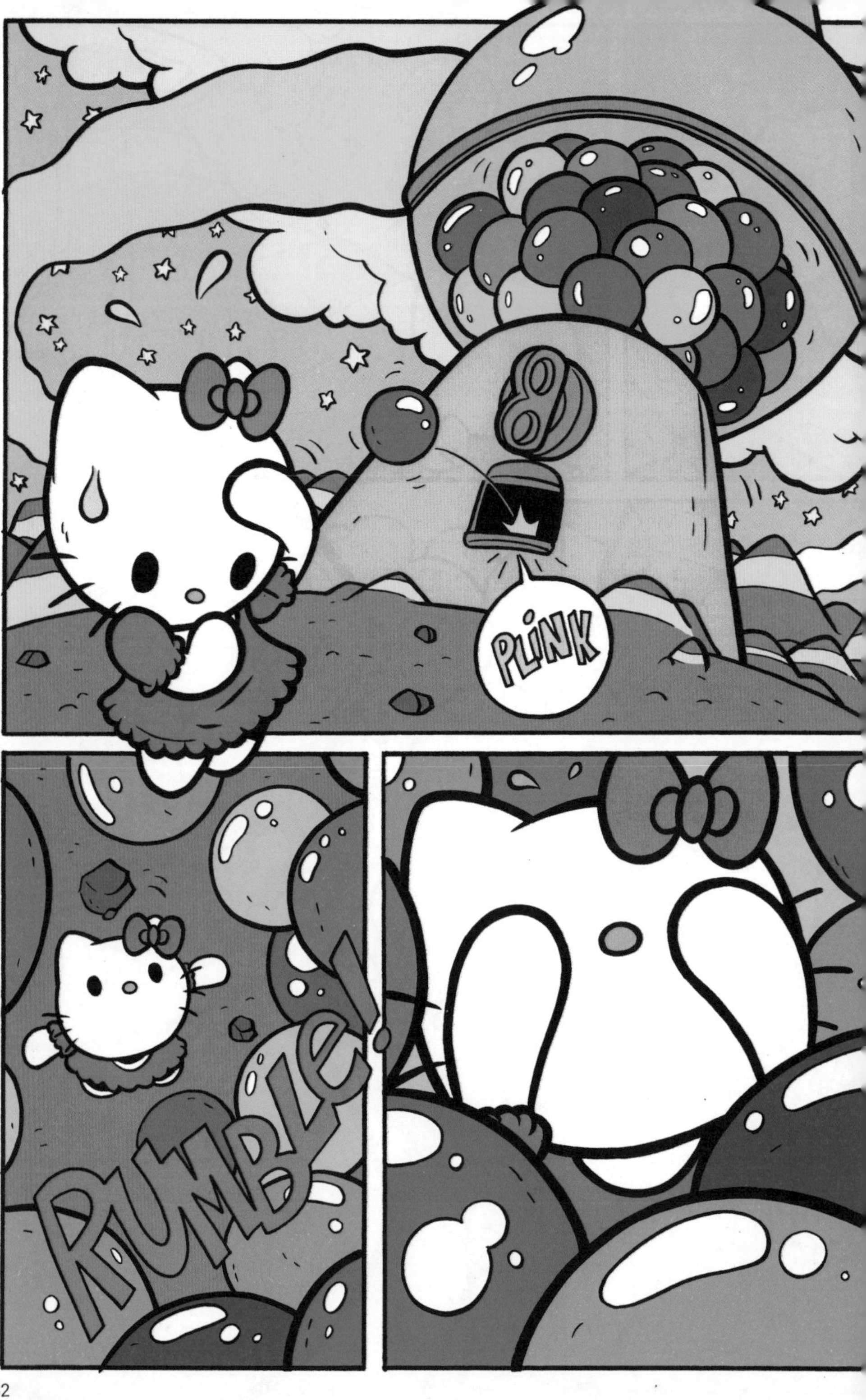
PLINK
RUMBLE!

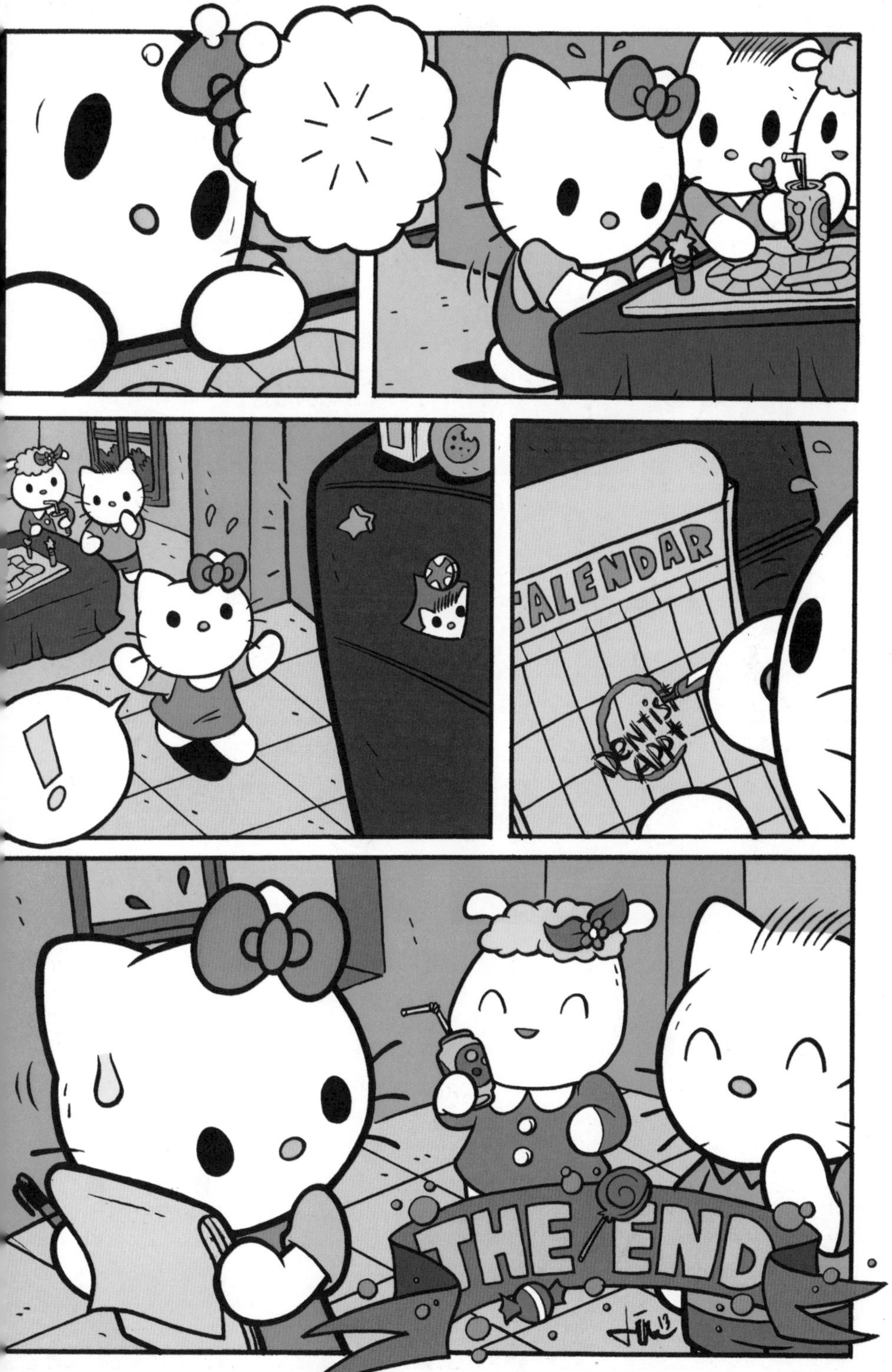
!
CALENDAR
DENTIST APPT
THE END

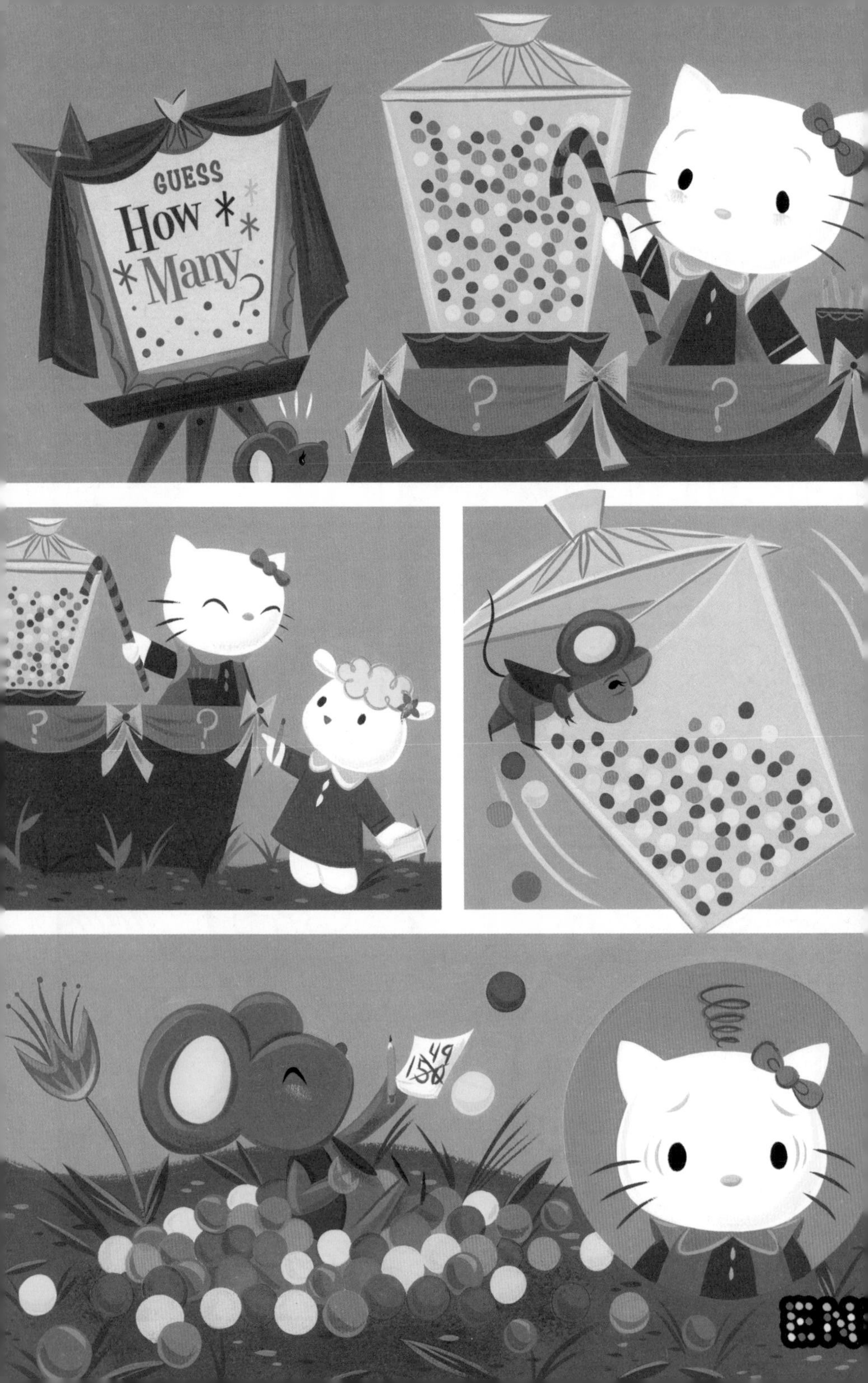
GUESS
How
Many
?
?
?
49
150

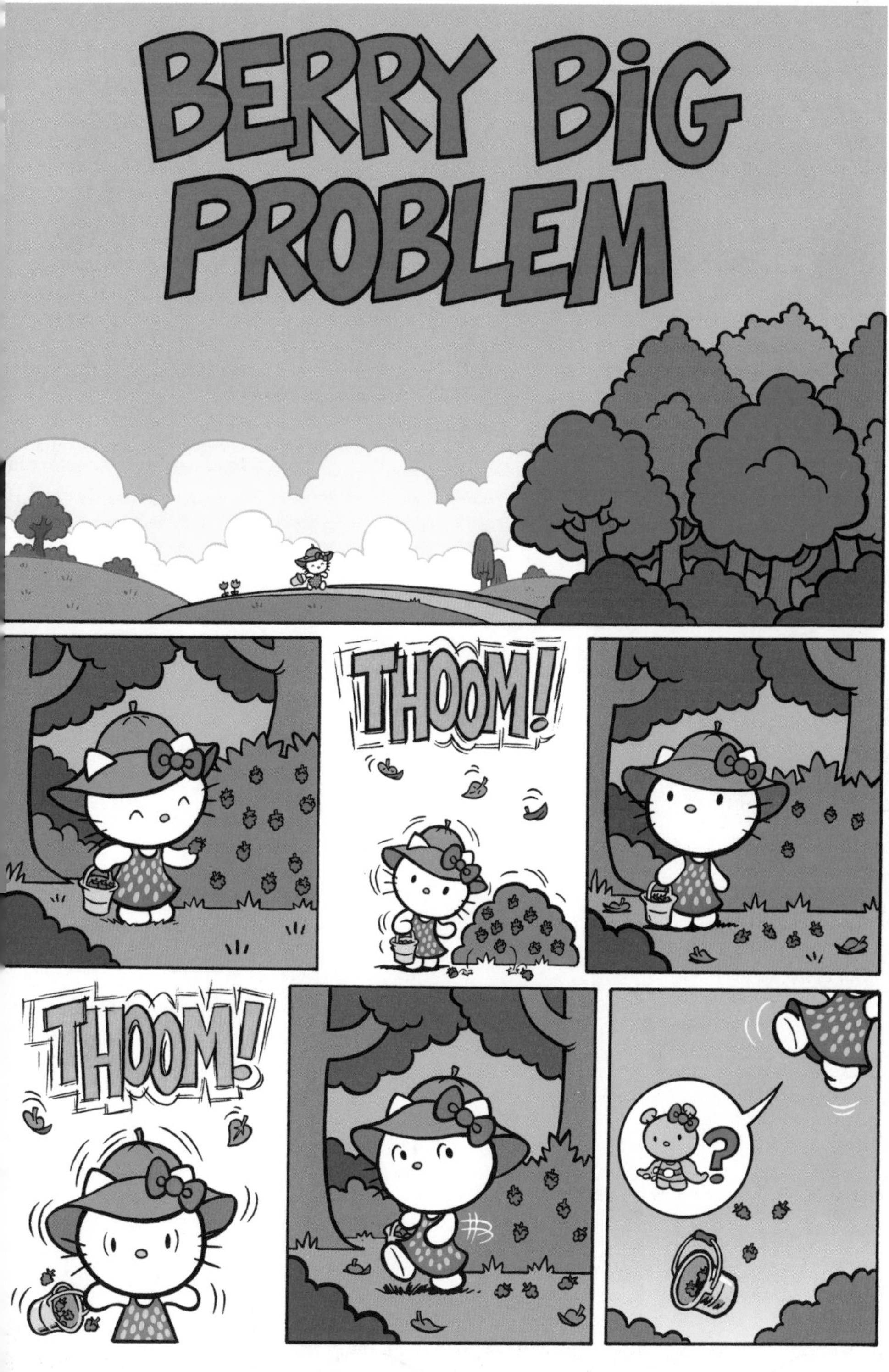
BERRY BIG PROBLEM
THOOM!
THOOM!
?

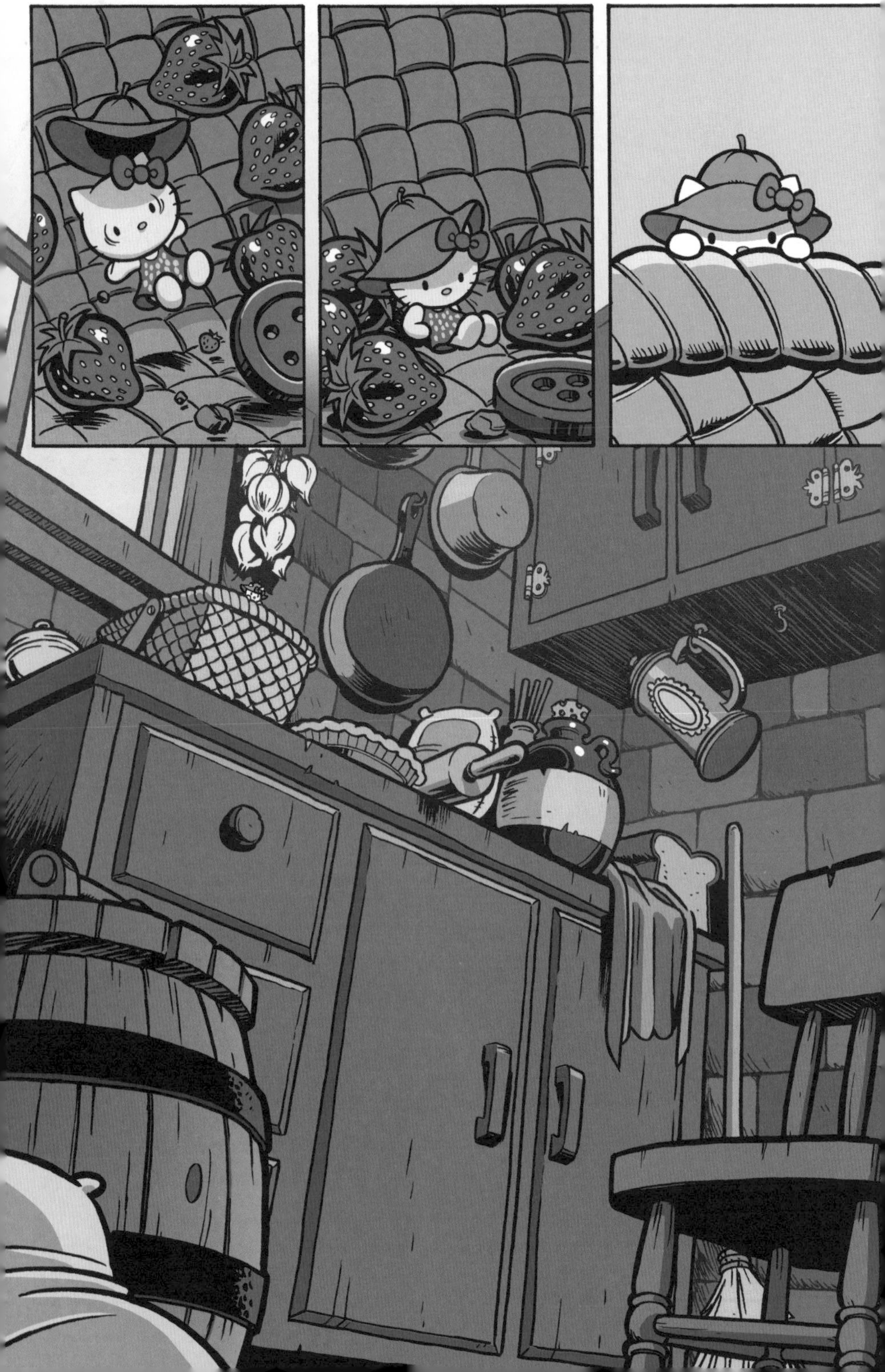

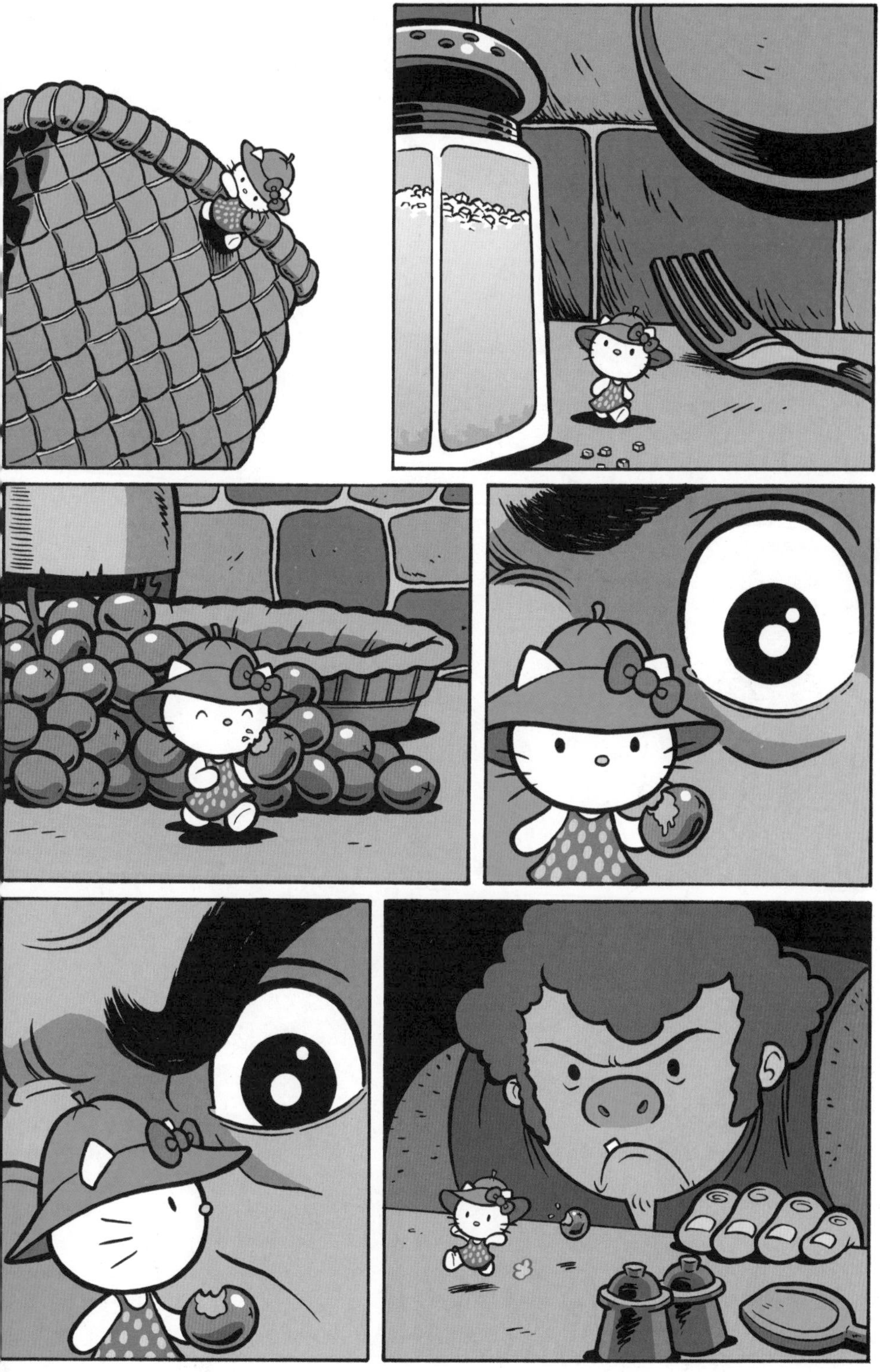

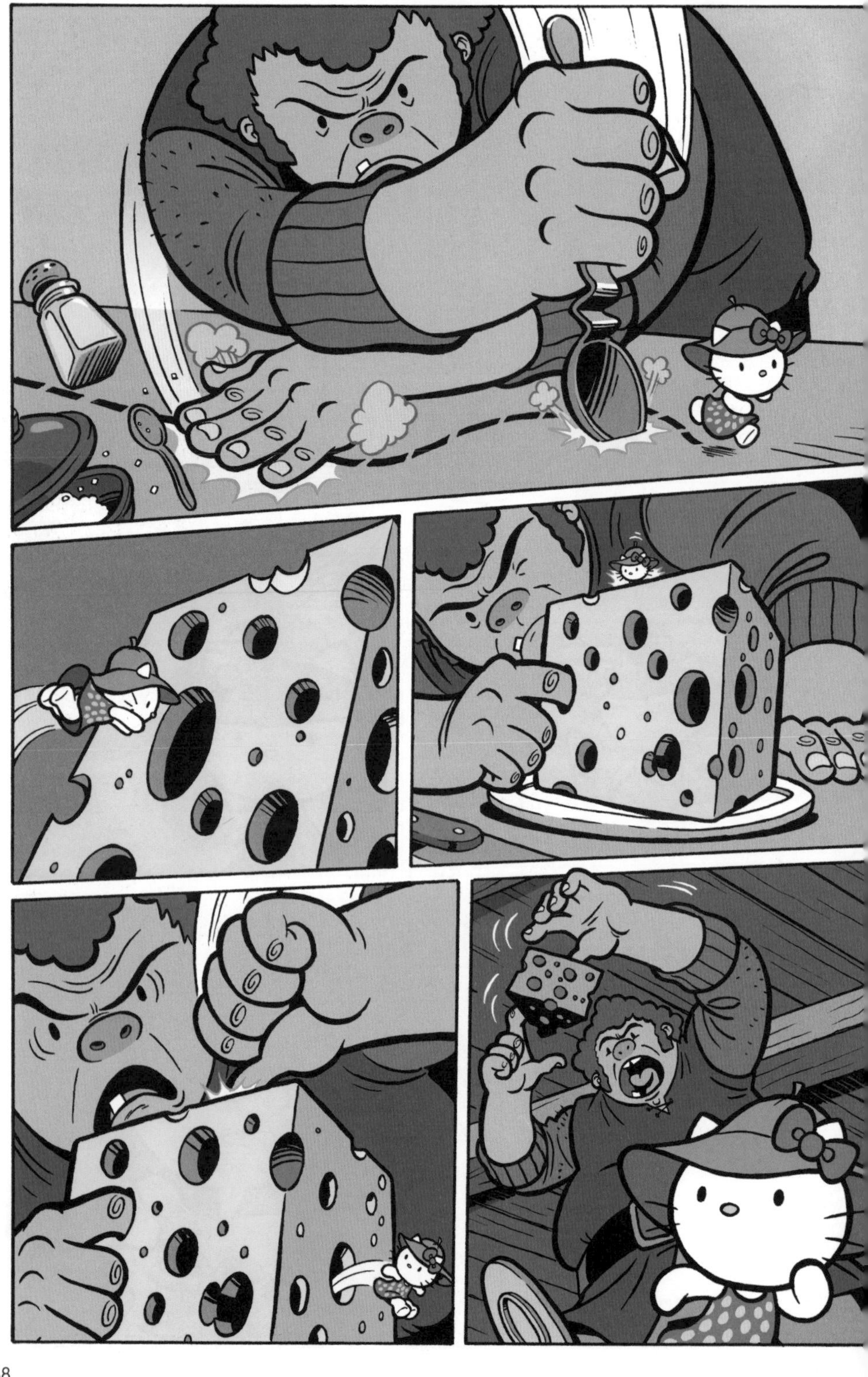

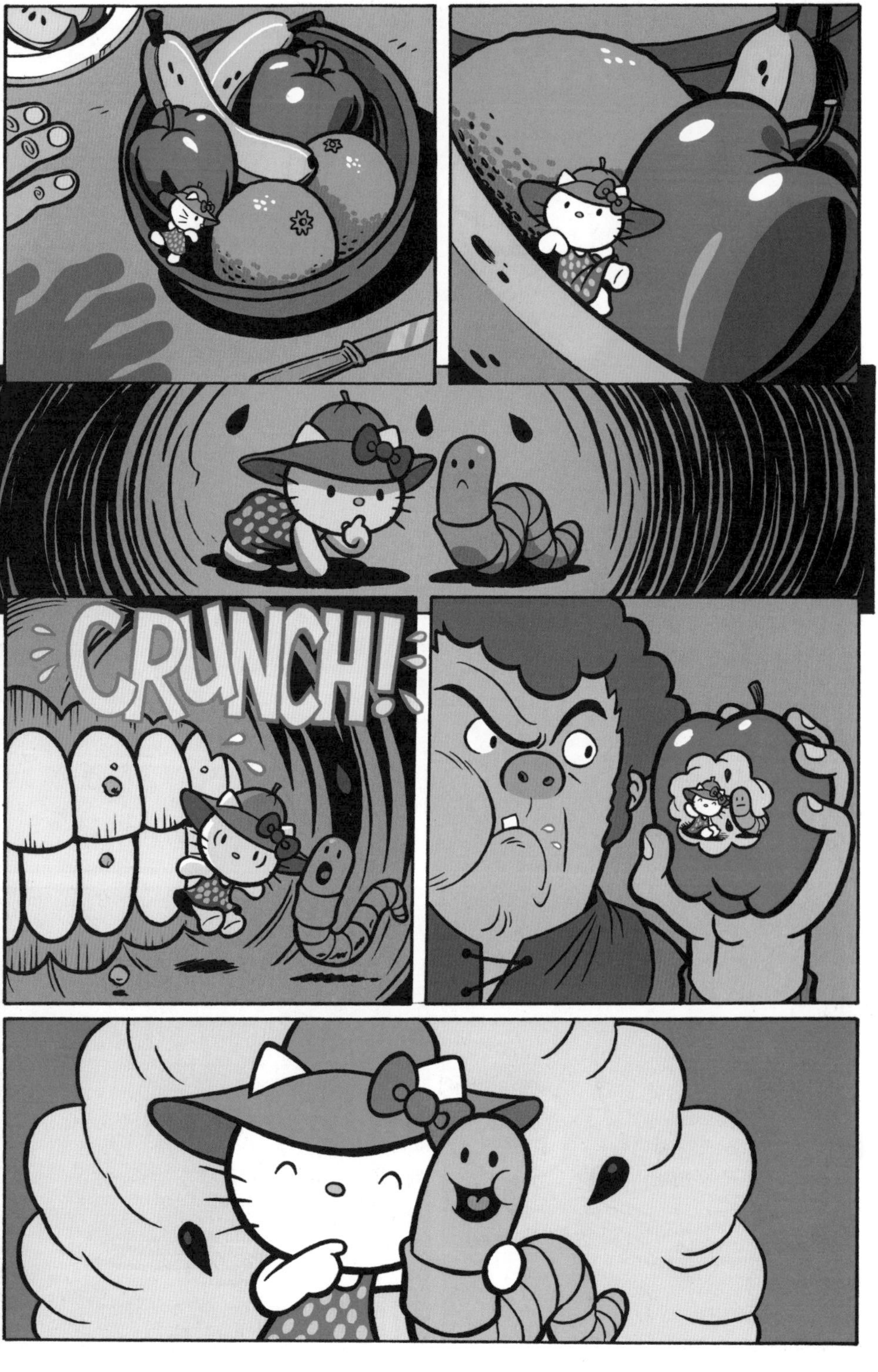
CRUNCH!

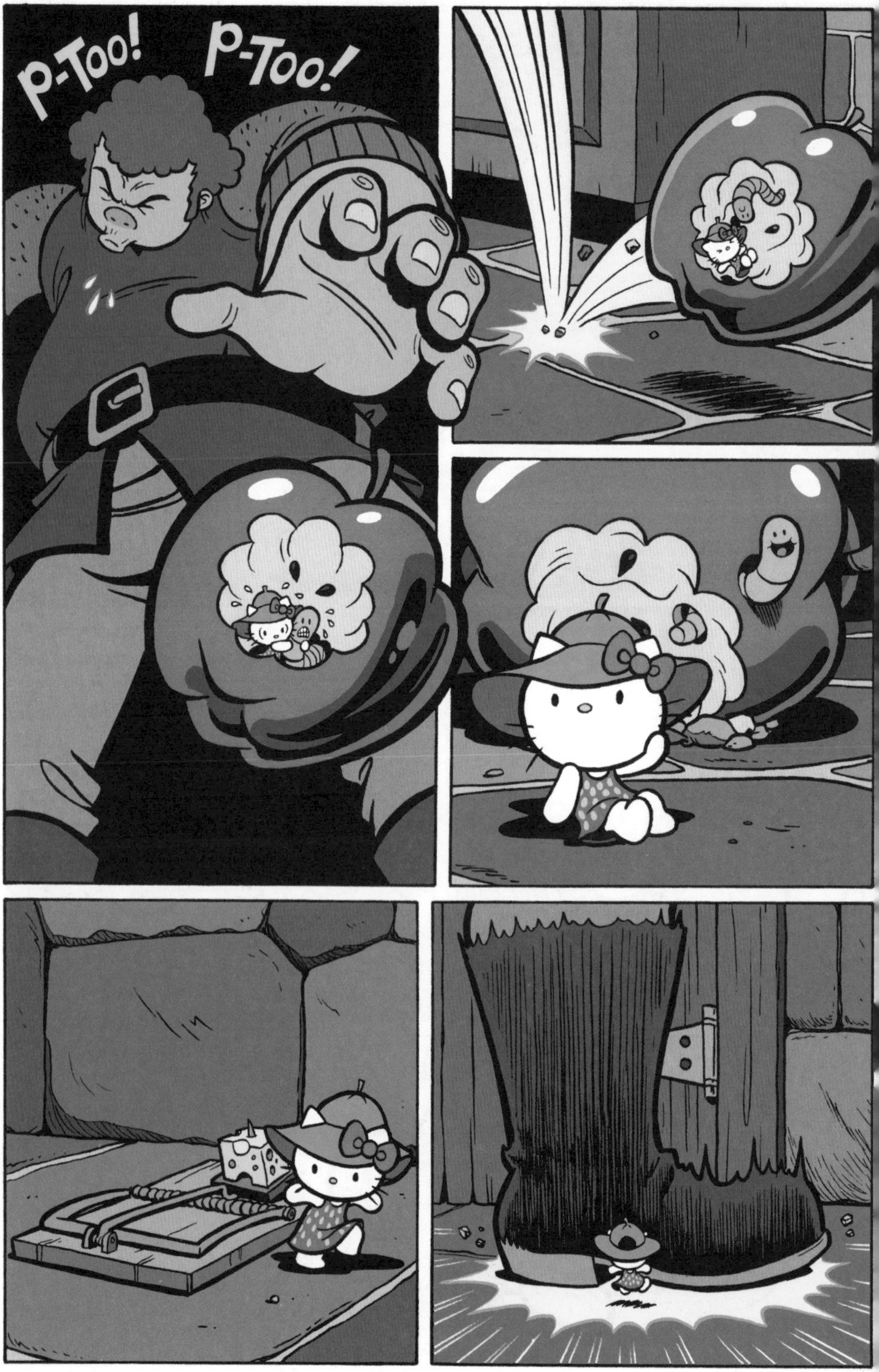
P-TOO!
P-TOO!

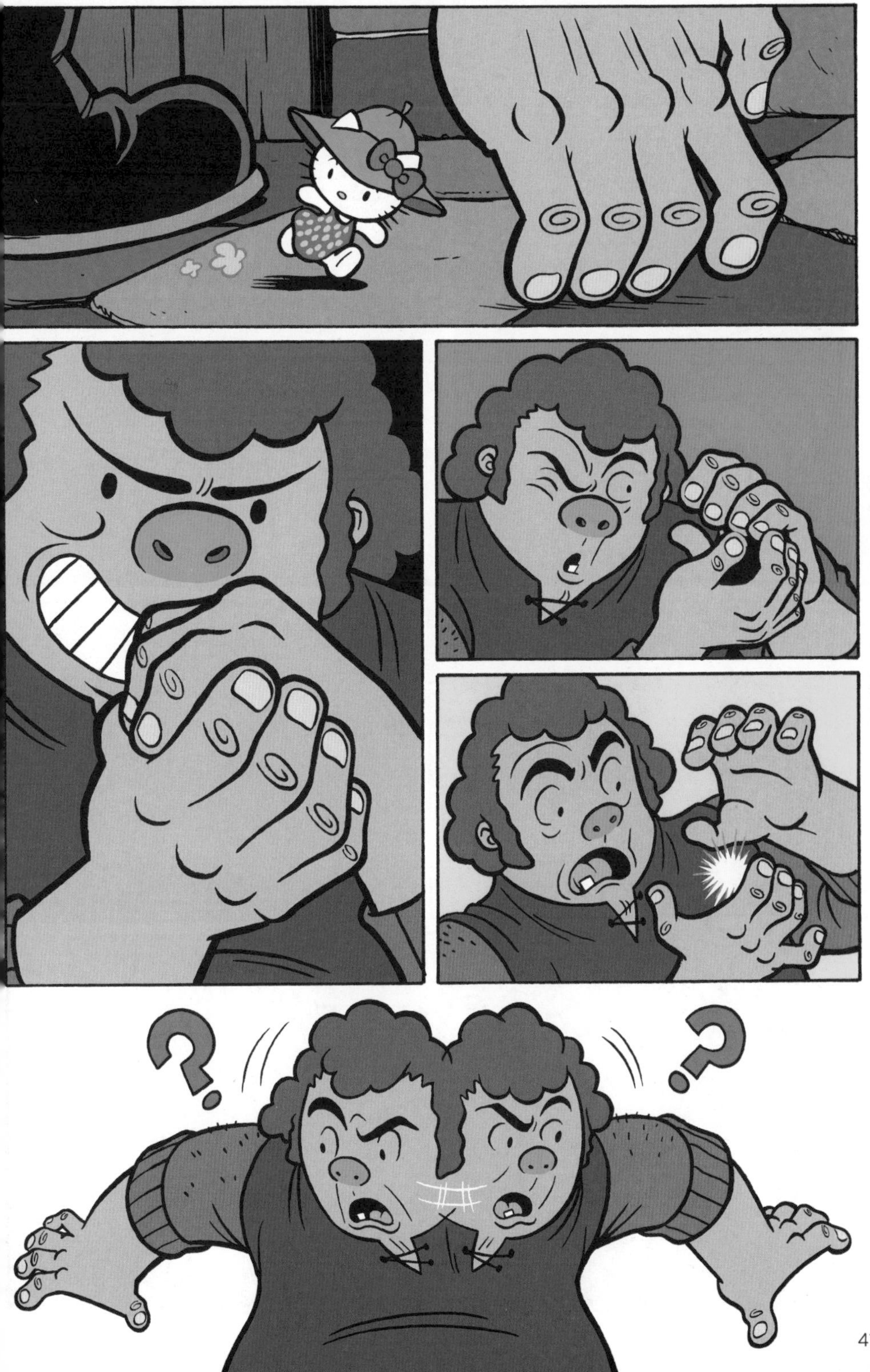

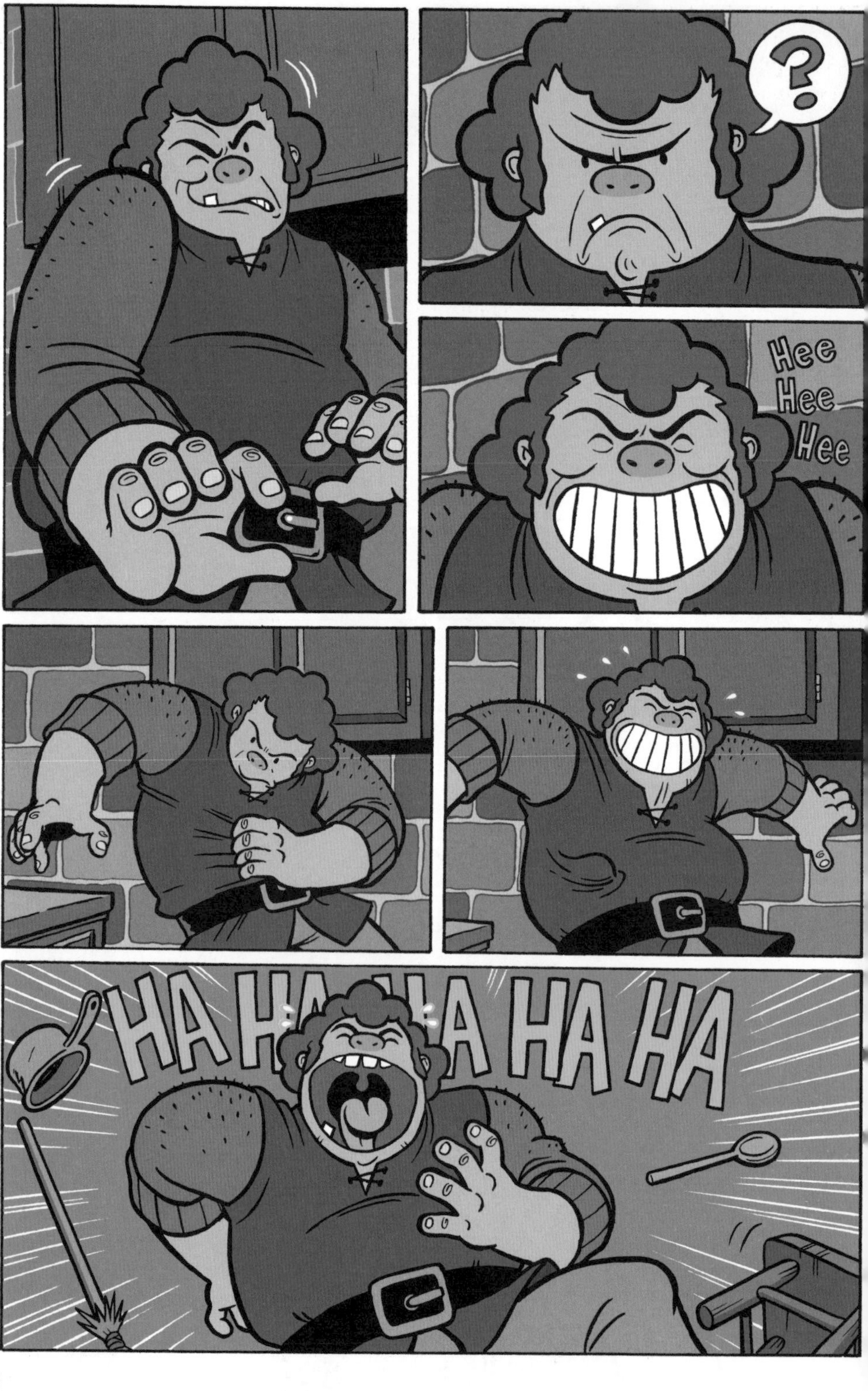
?
Hee
Hee
Hee
HA HA HA HA HA

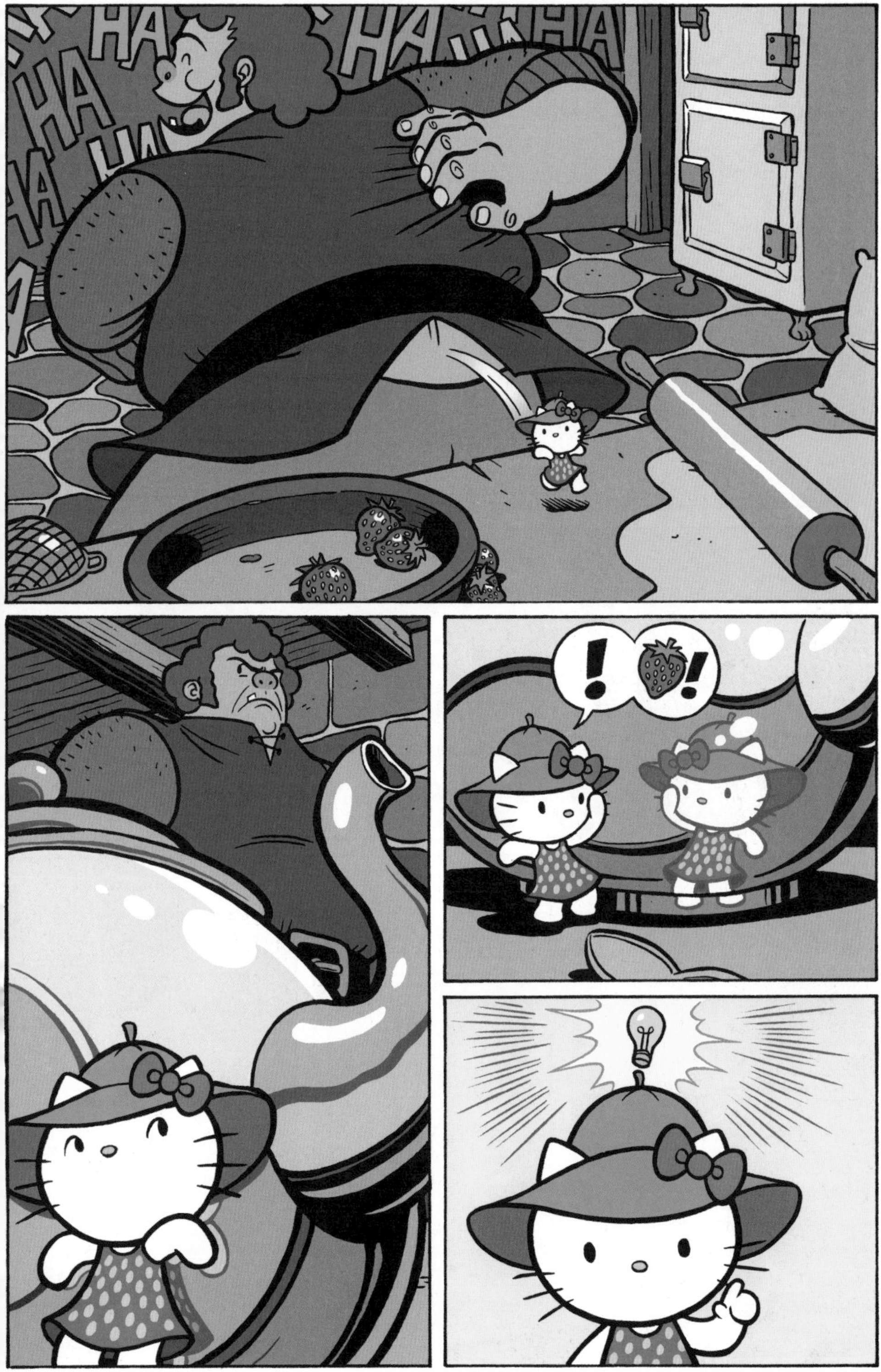
HA HA HA HA
HA HA HA HA HA
!
!

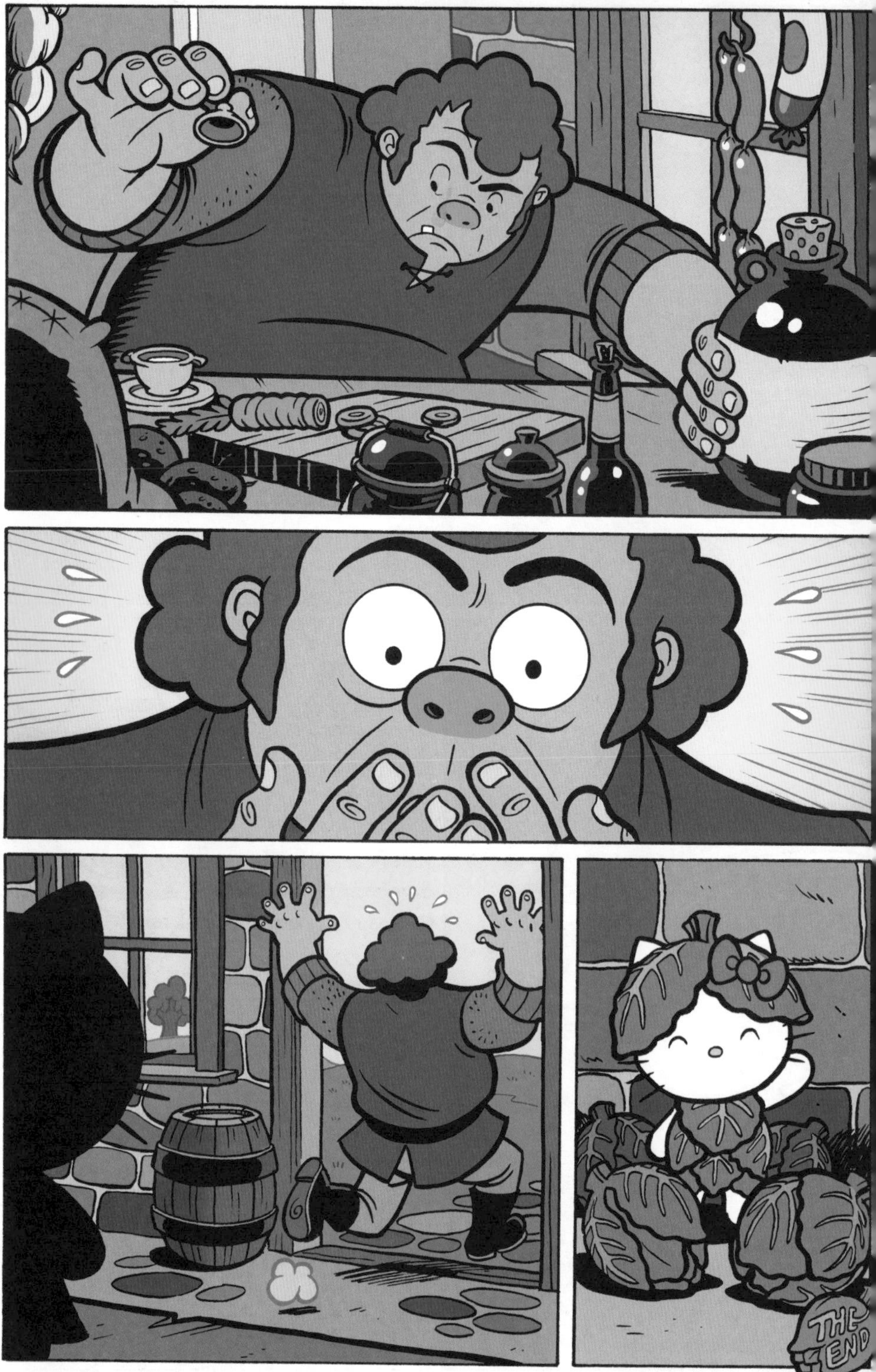
THE END

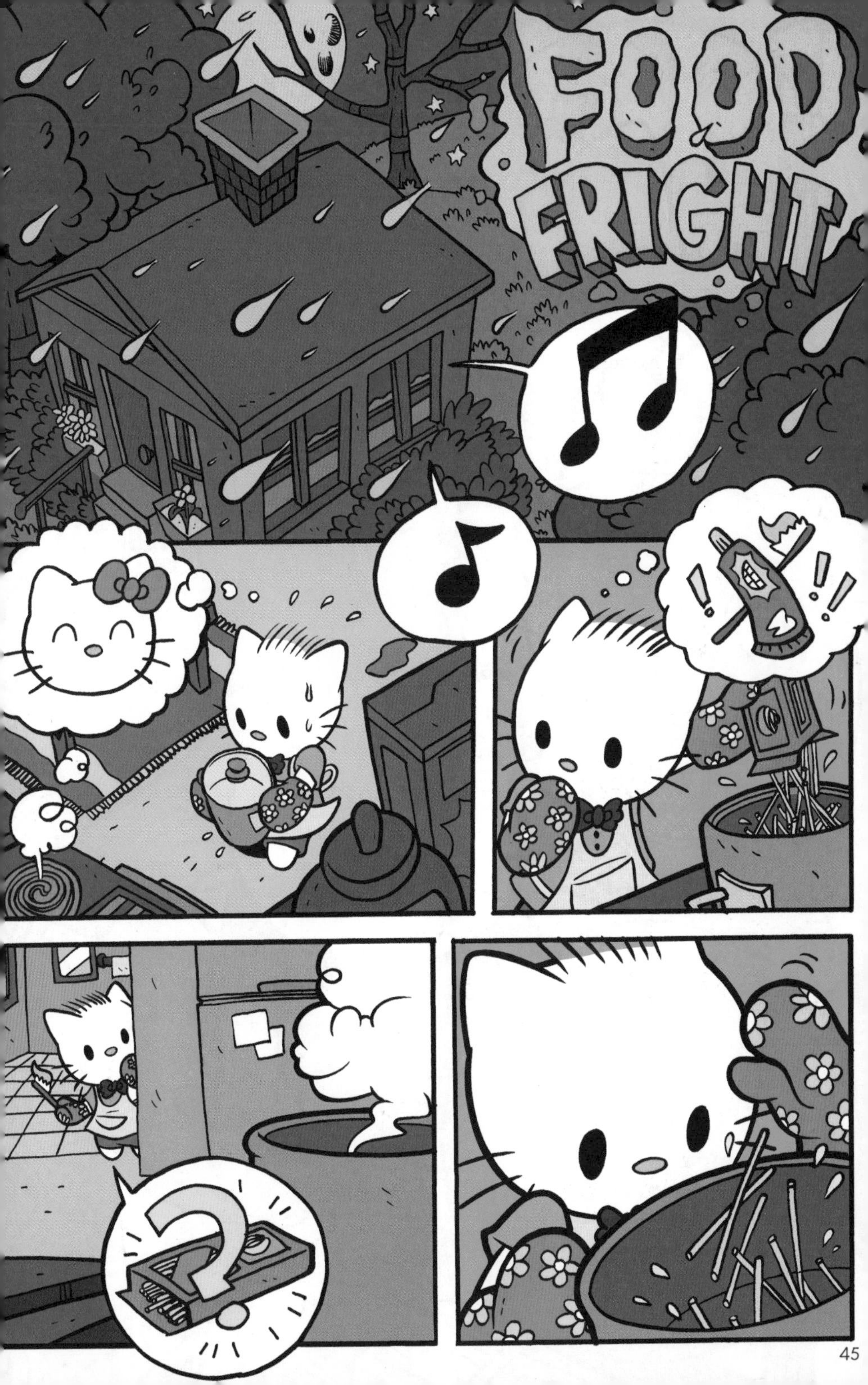
FOOD
FRIGHT

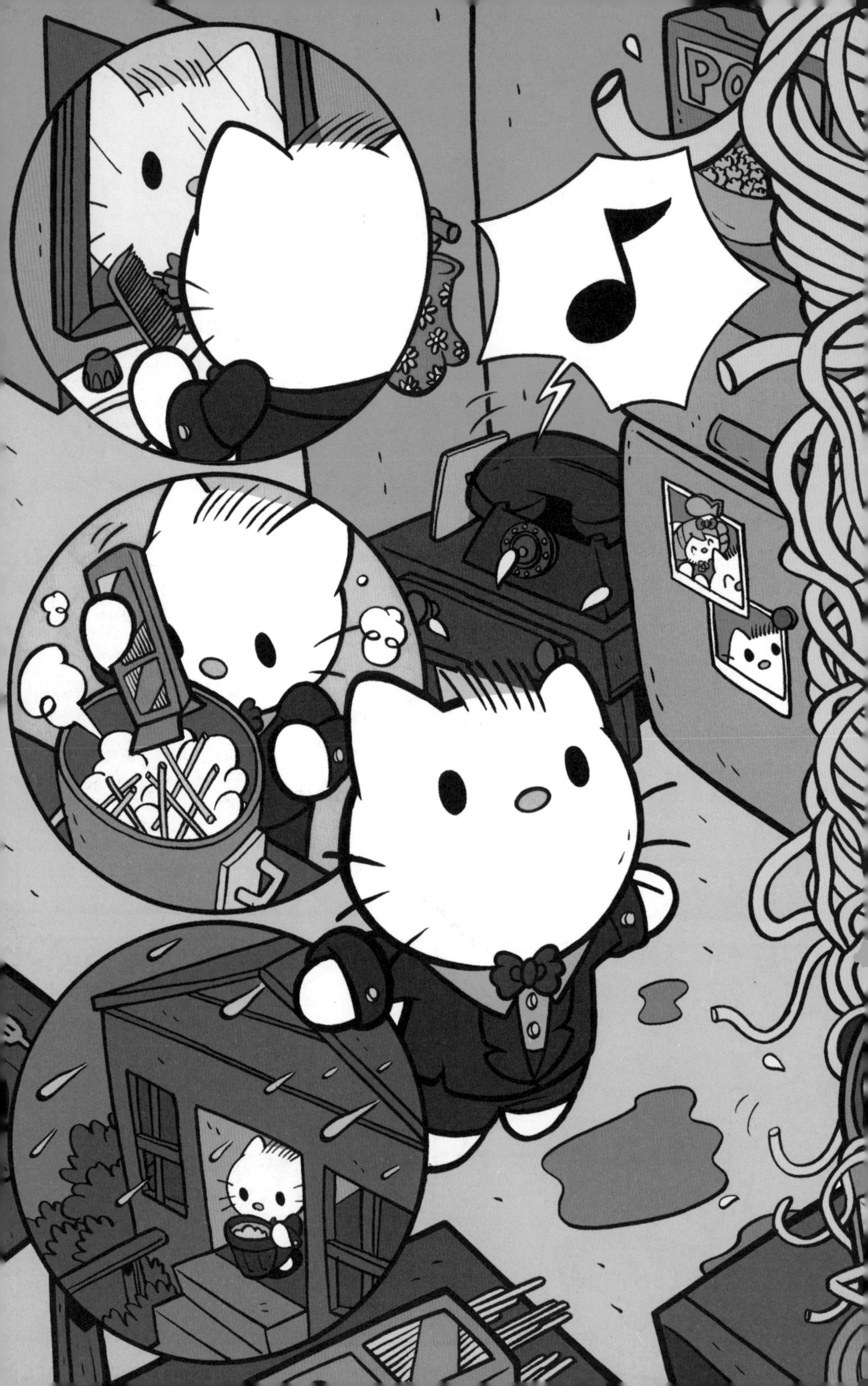

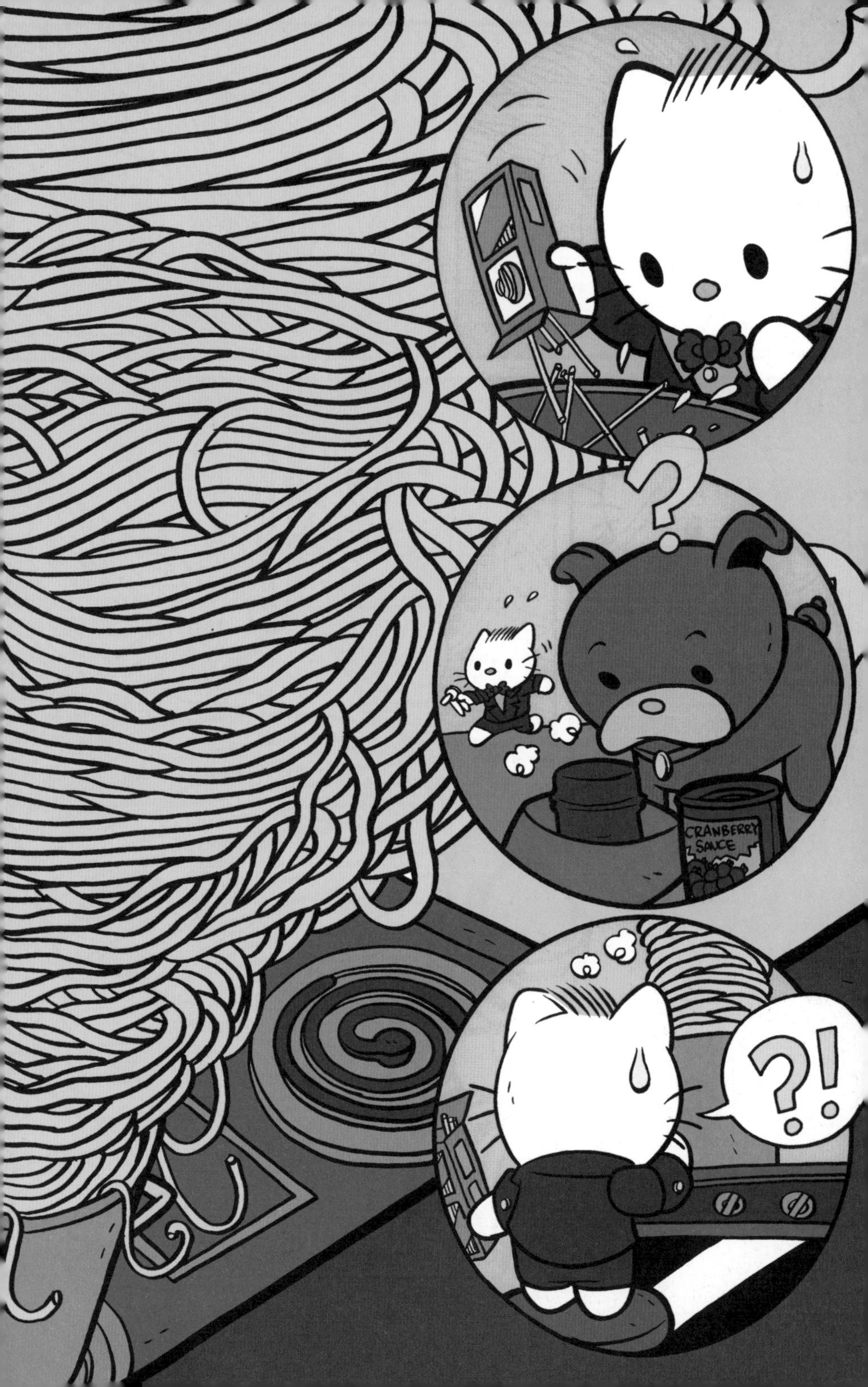
CRANBERRY SAUCE
?!

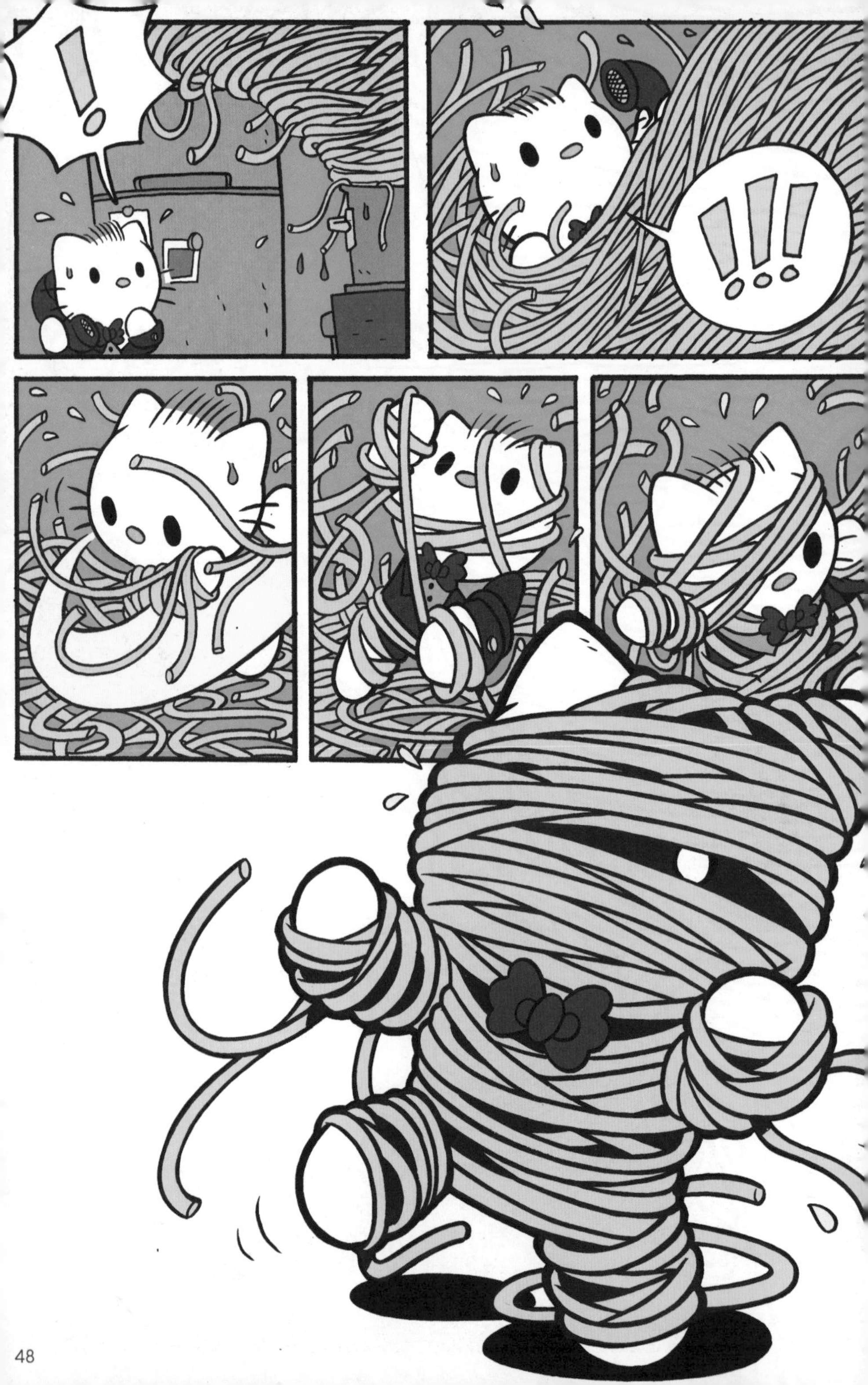
!
!!!

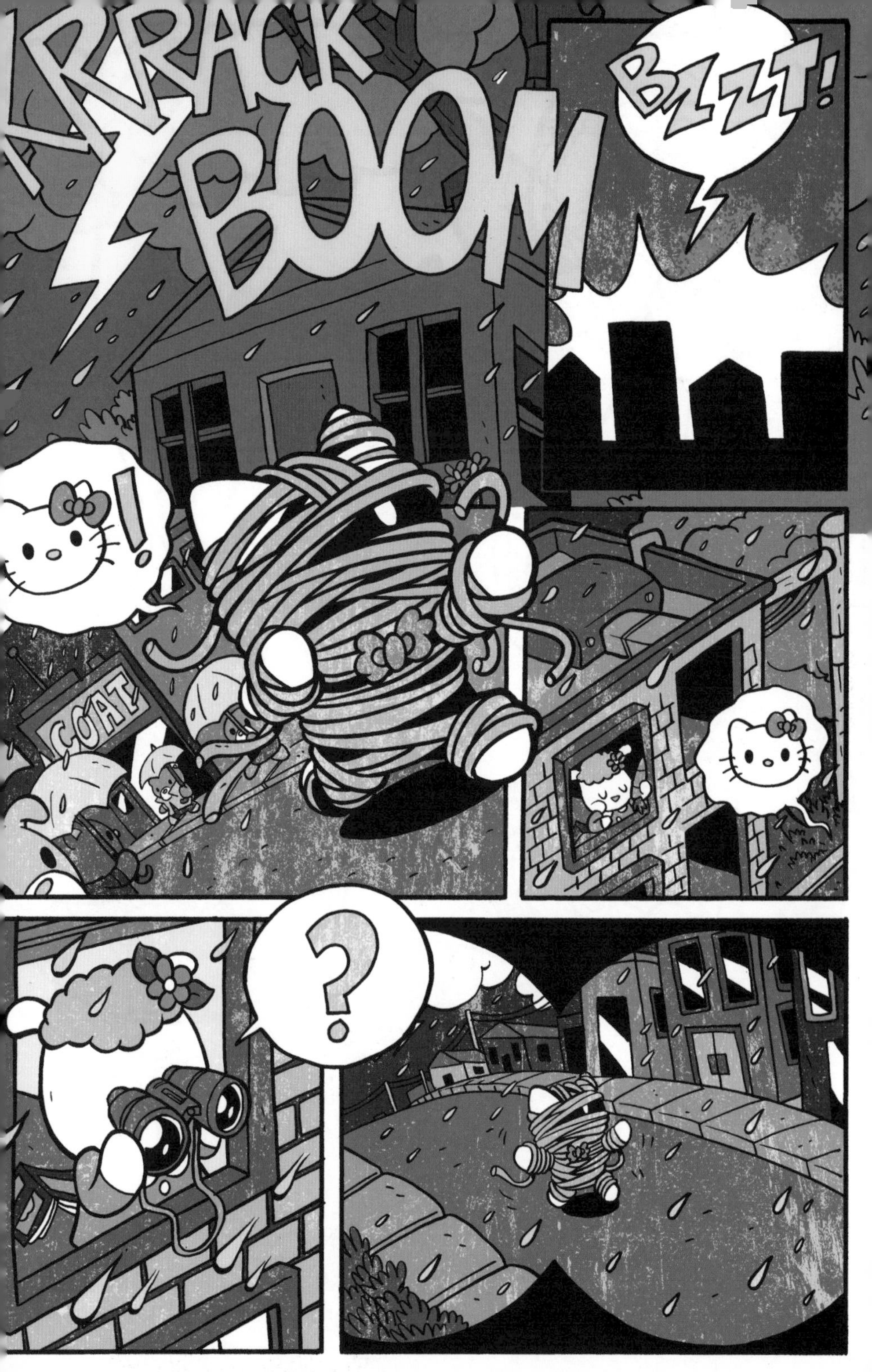
KRRACK
BOOM
BZZT!
!
COAT
?

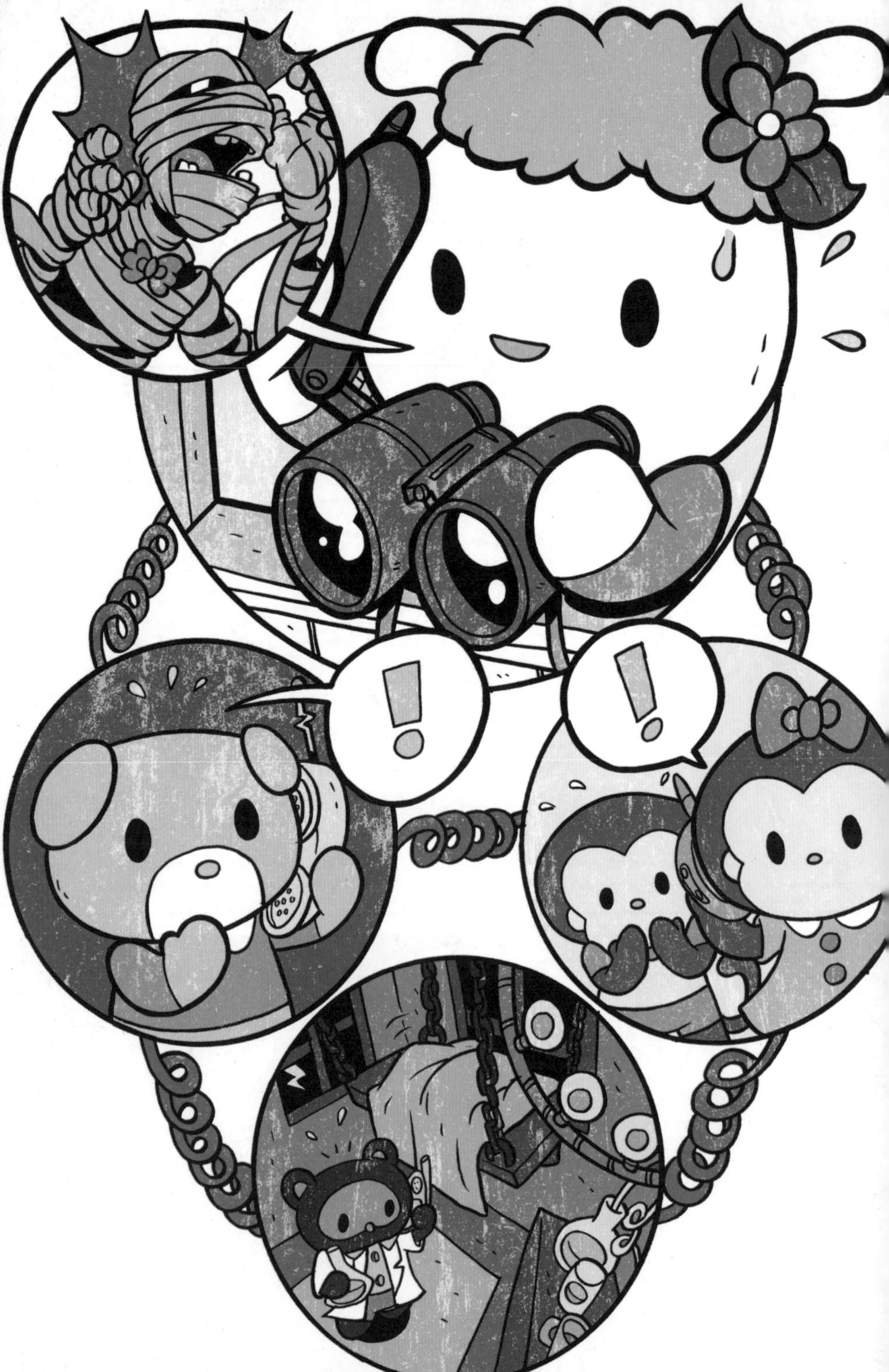
!
!

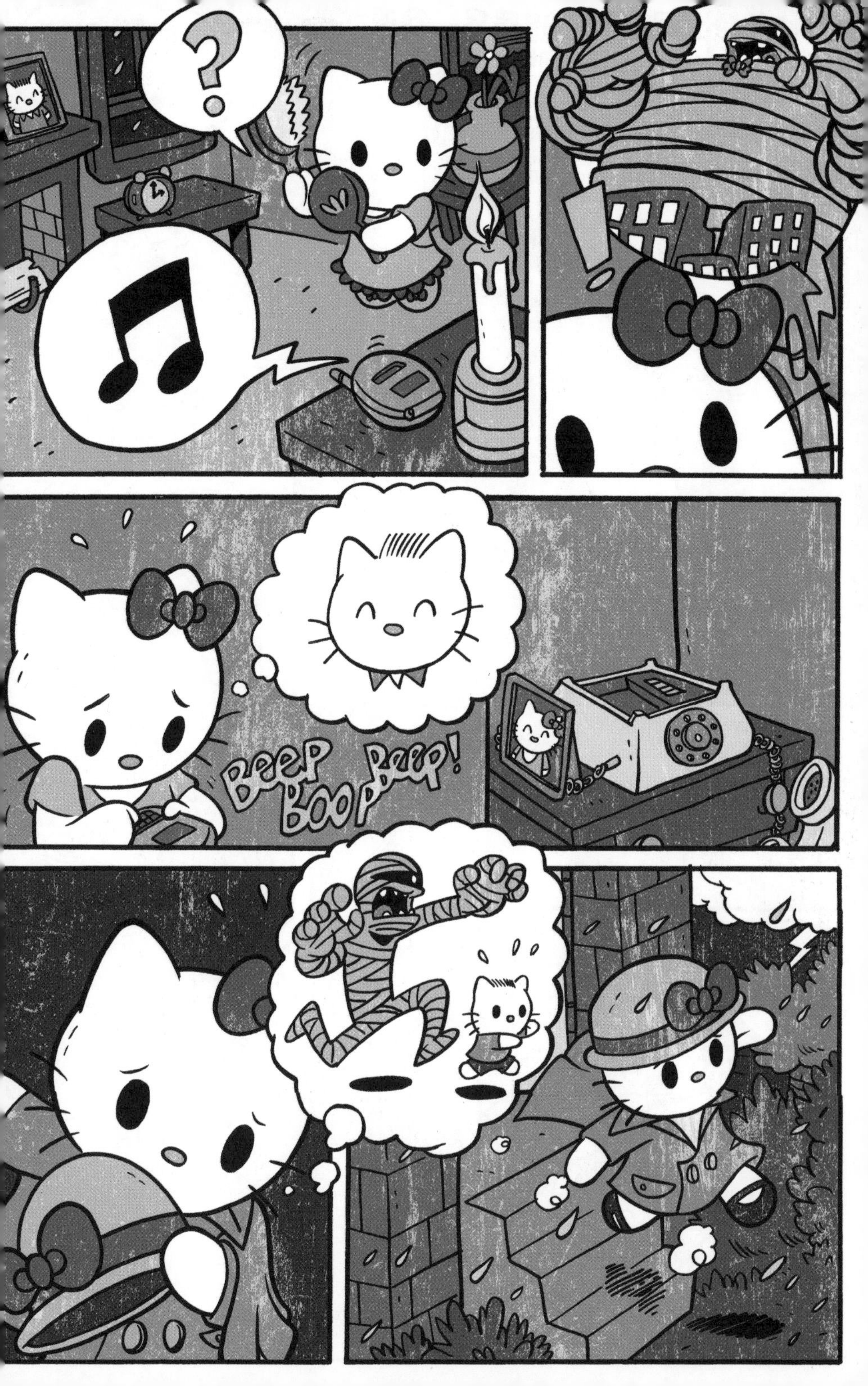
BEEP BOOP BEEP!

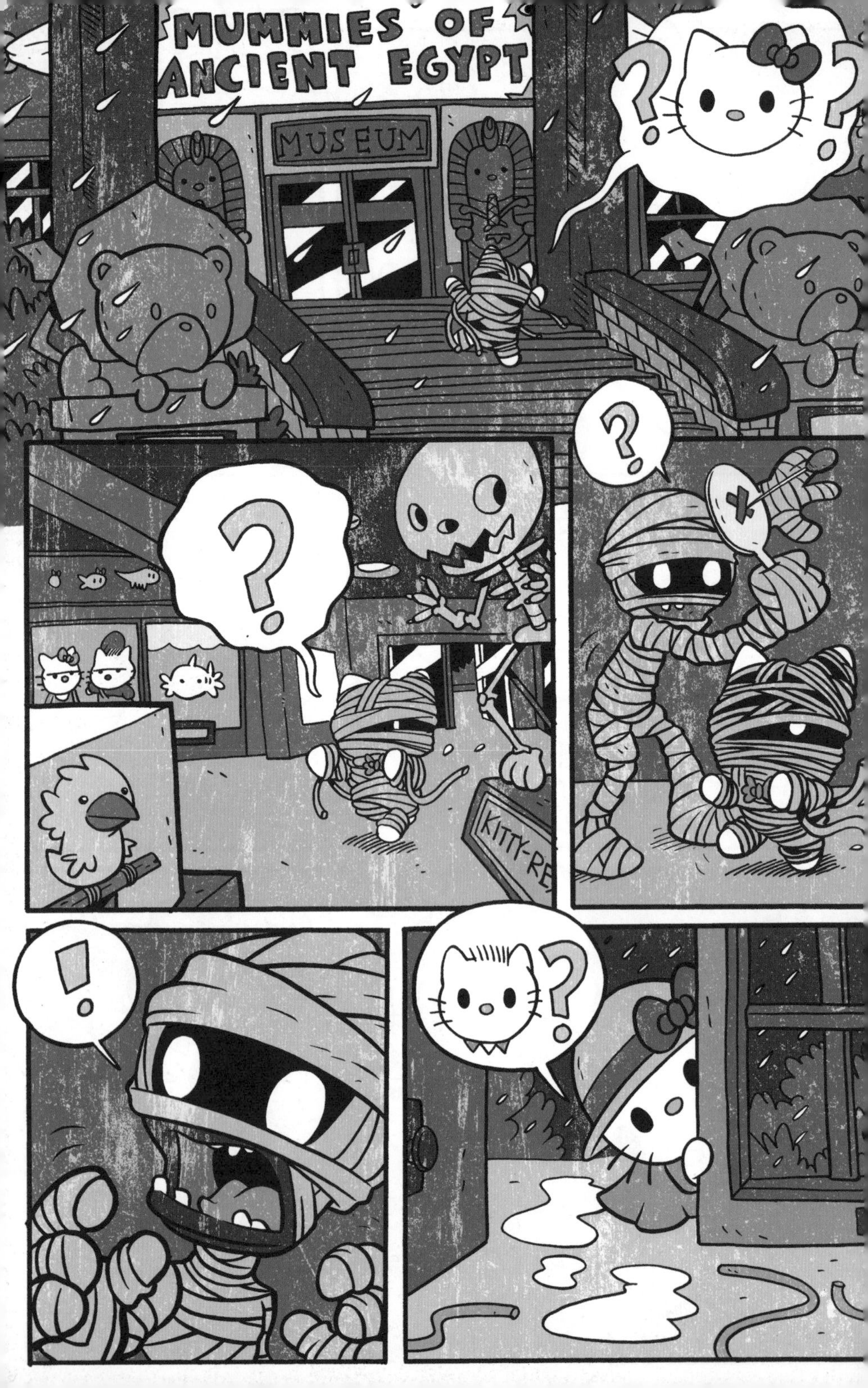
MUMMIES OF ANCIENT EGYPT
MUSEUM
?
?
KITTY-RE
?
!
?

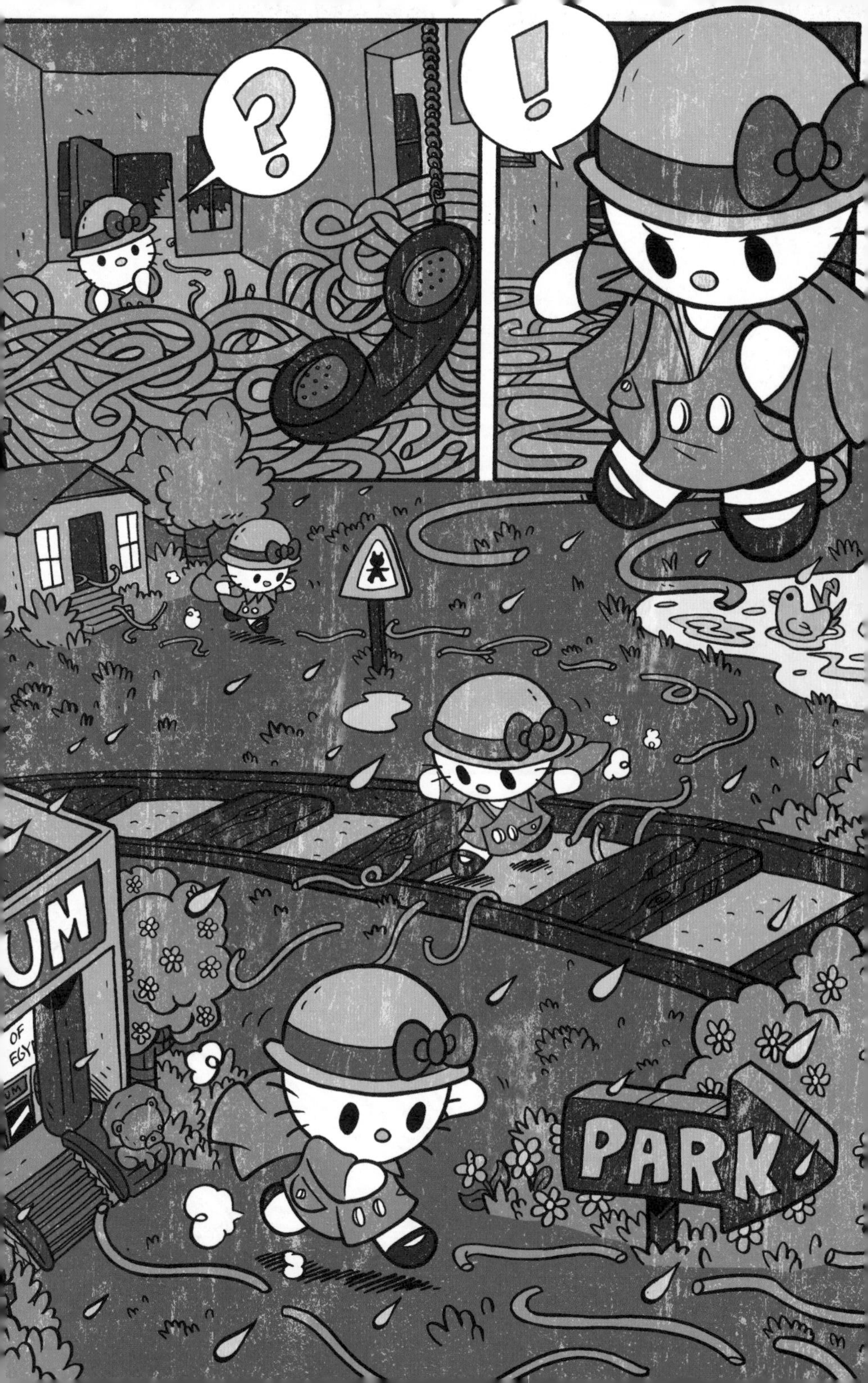
?
!
UM
OF
EGY
PARK

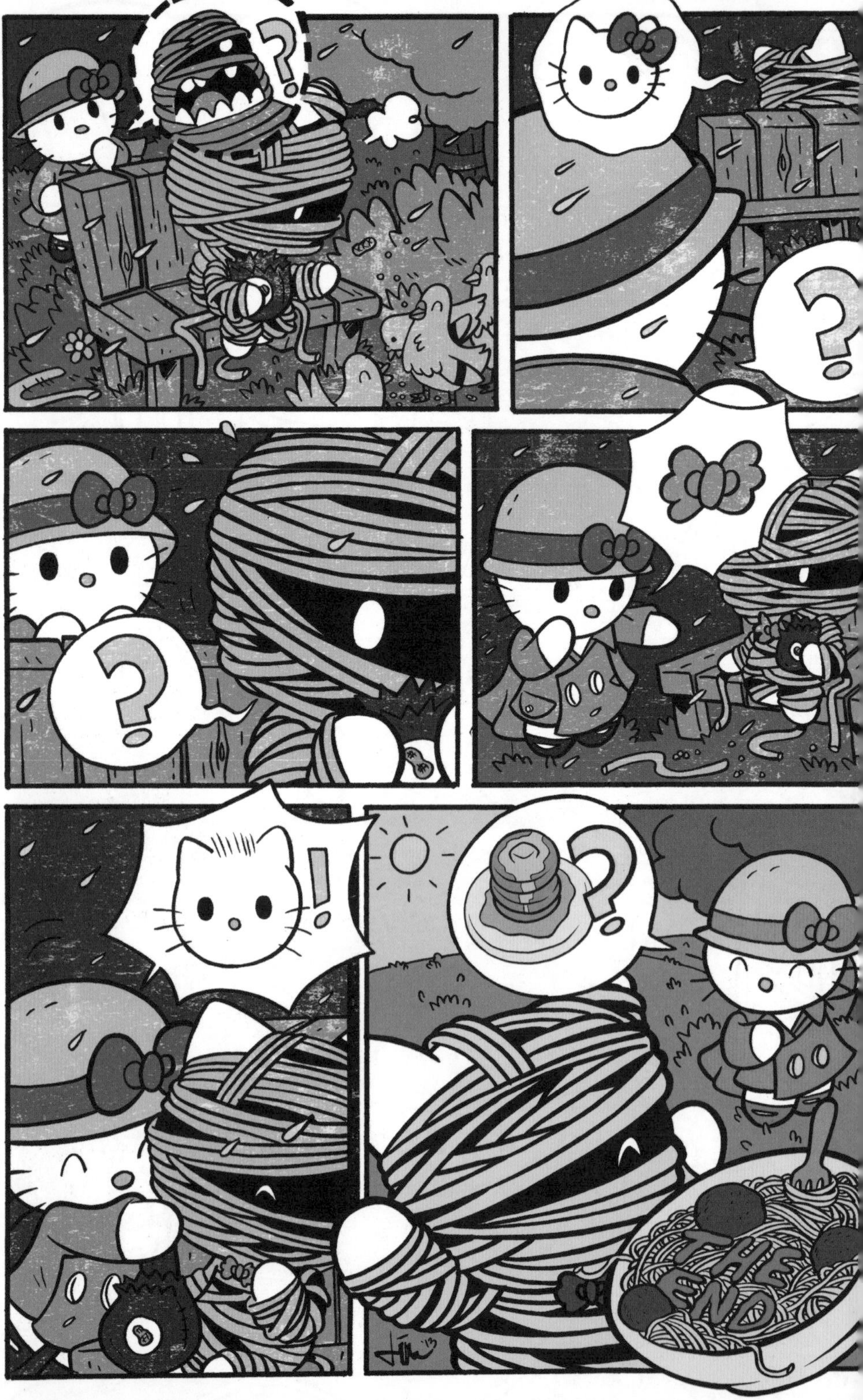
?
?
?
!
?
THE END

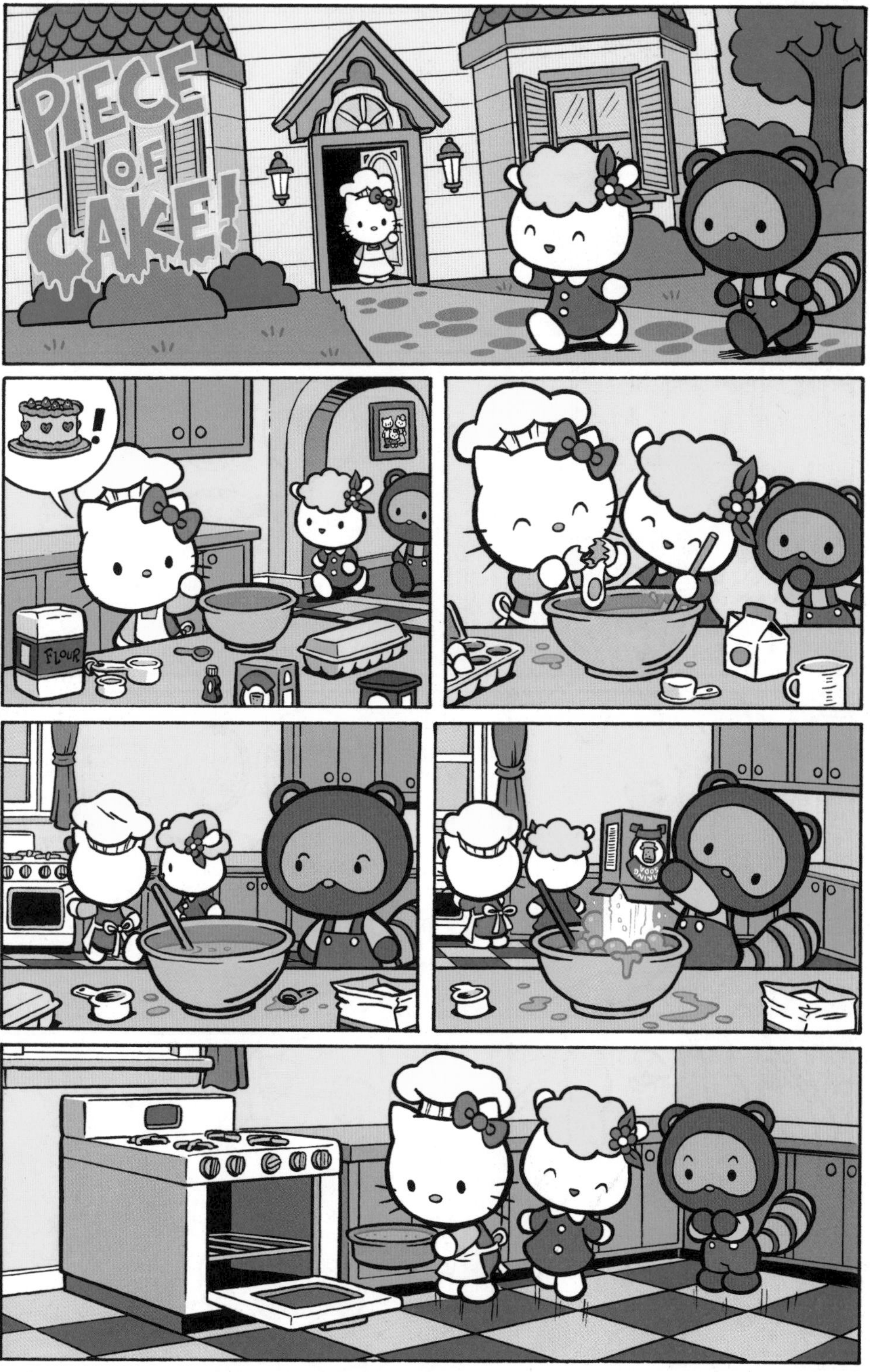
PIECE OF CAKE!
FLOUR

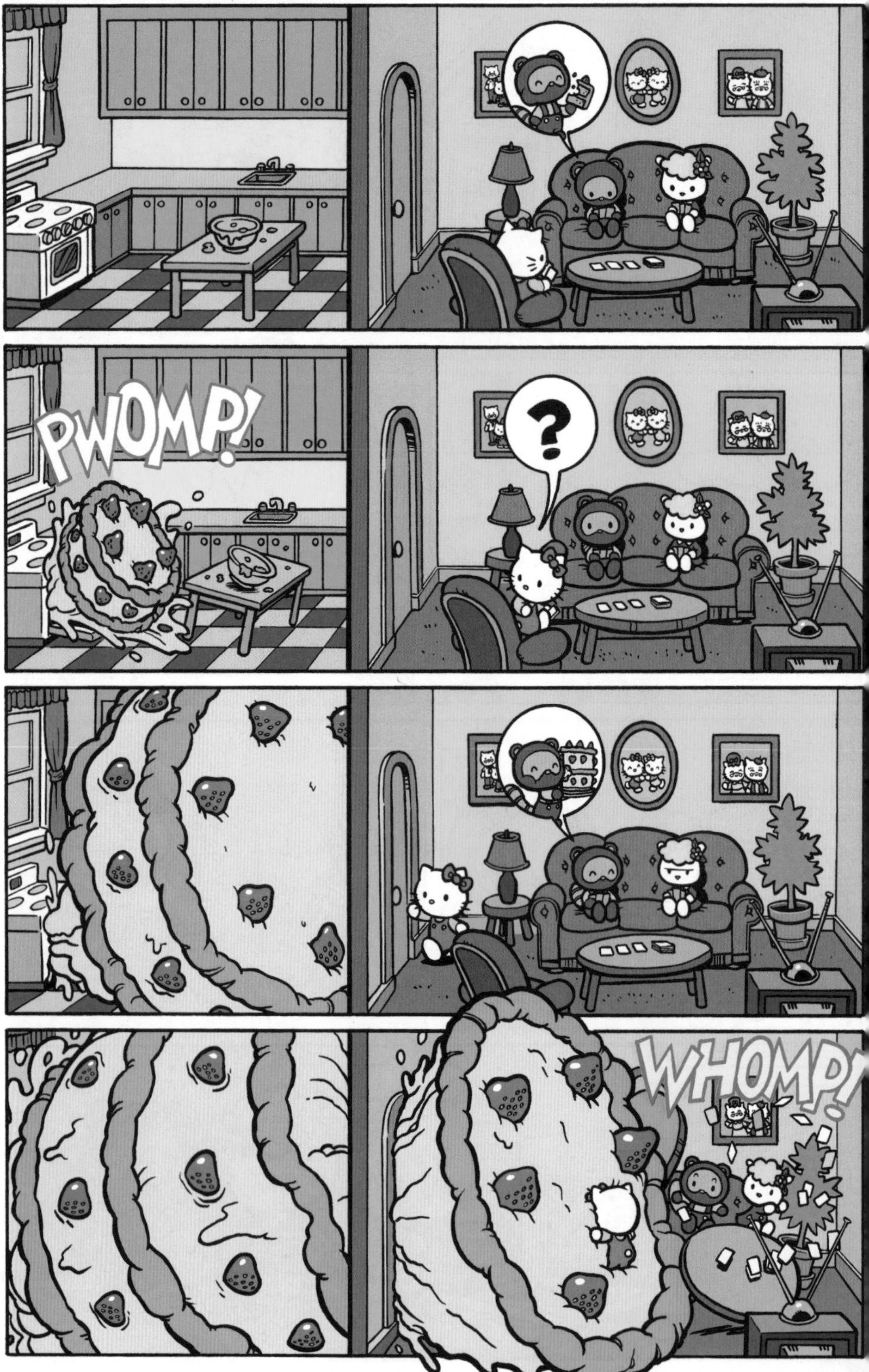
PWOMP!
?
WHOMP!

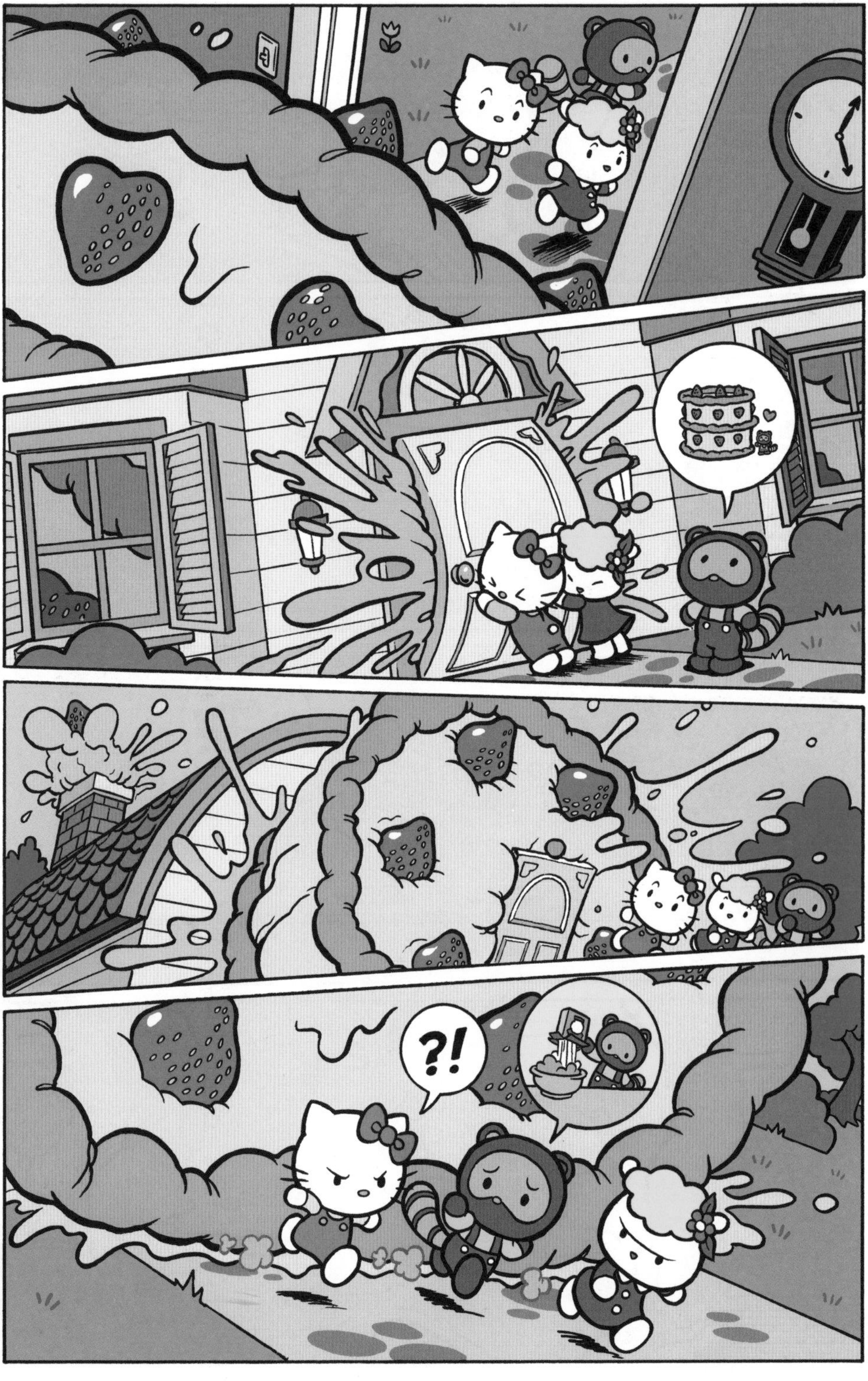
?!

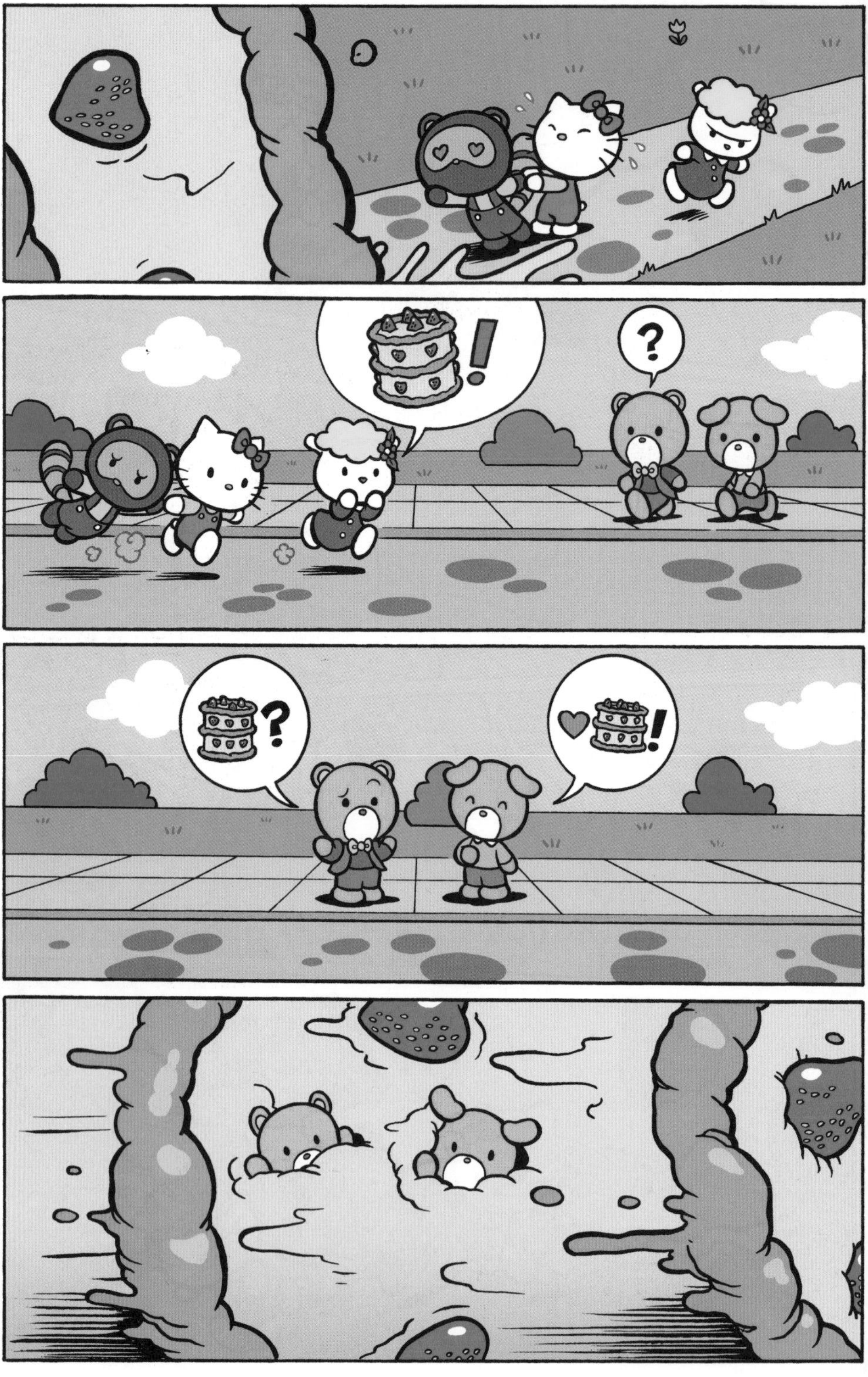
!
?
?
!

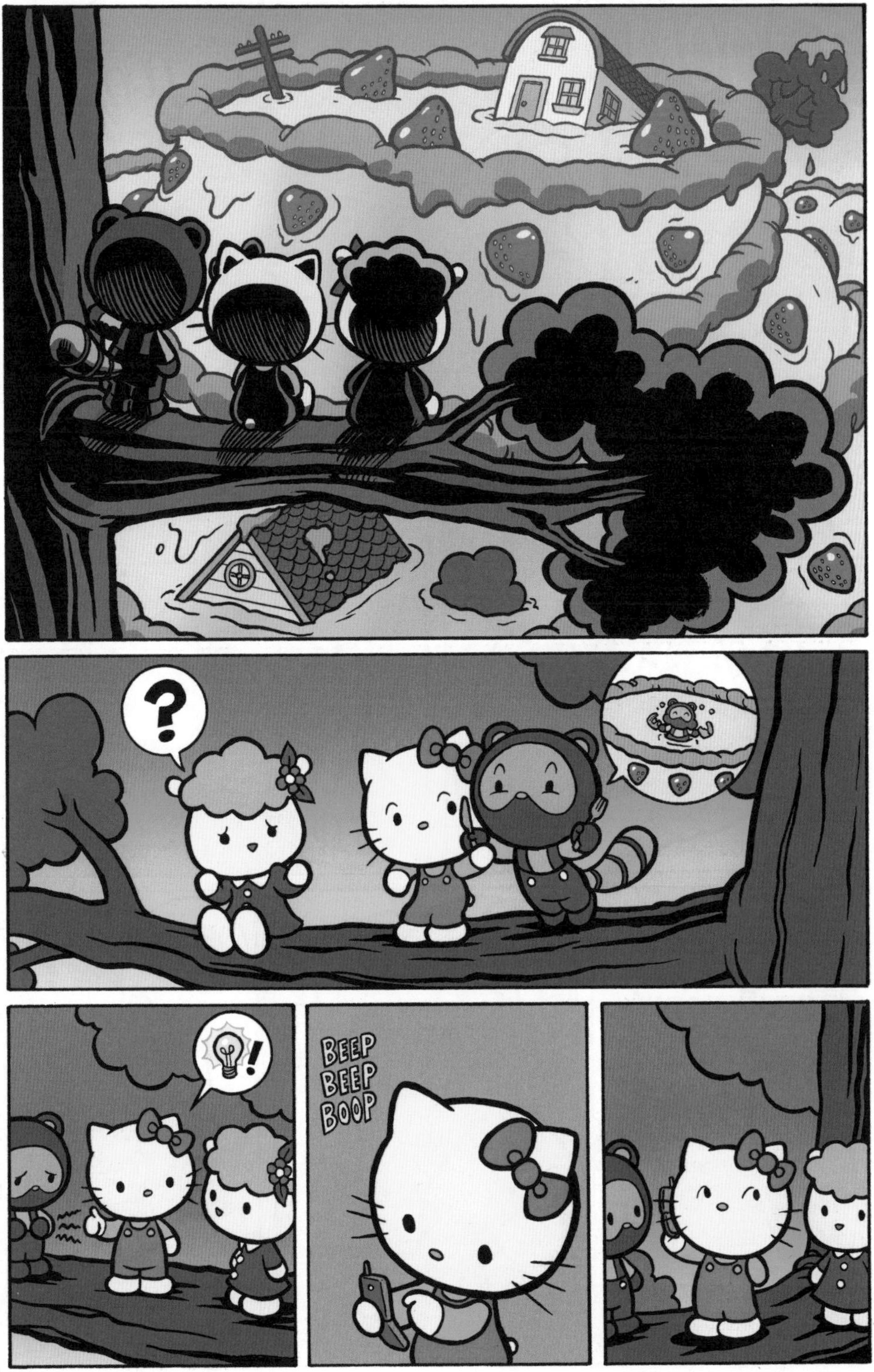
?
!
BEEP
BEEP
BOOP

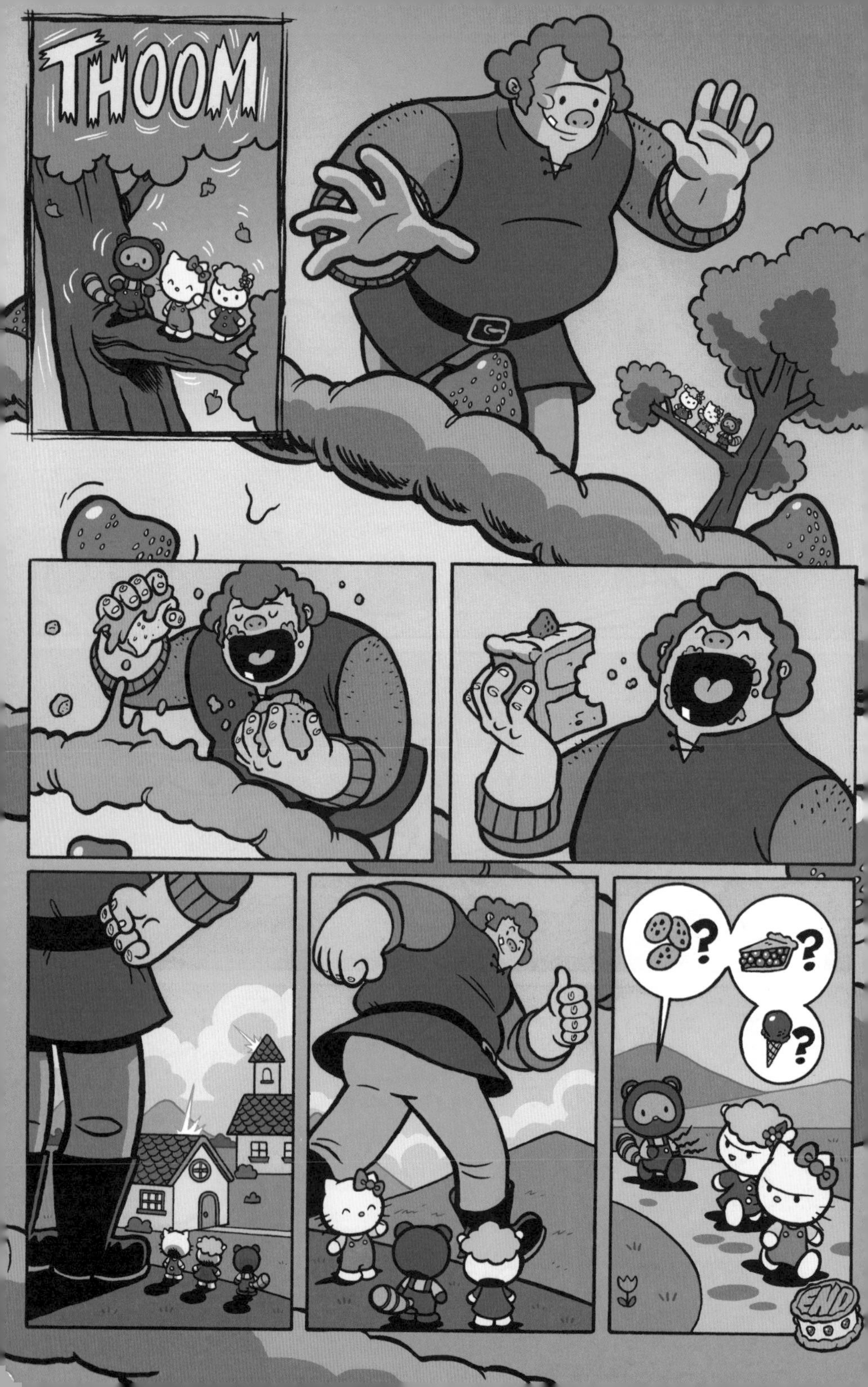
THOOM
?
?
?
END

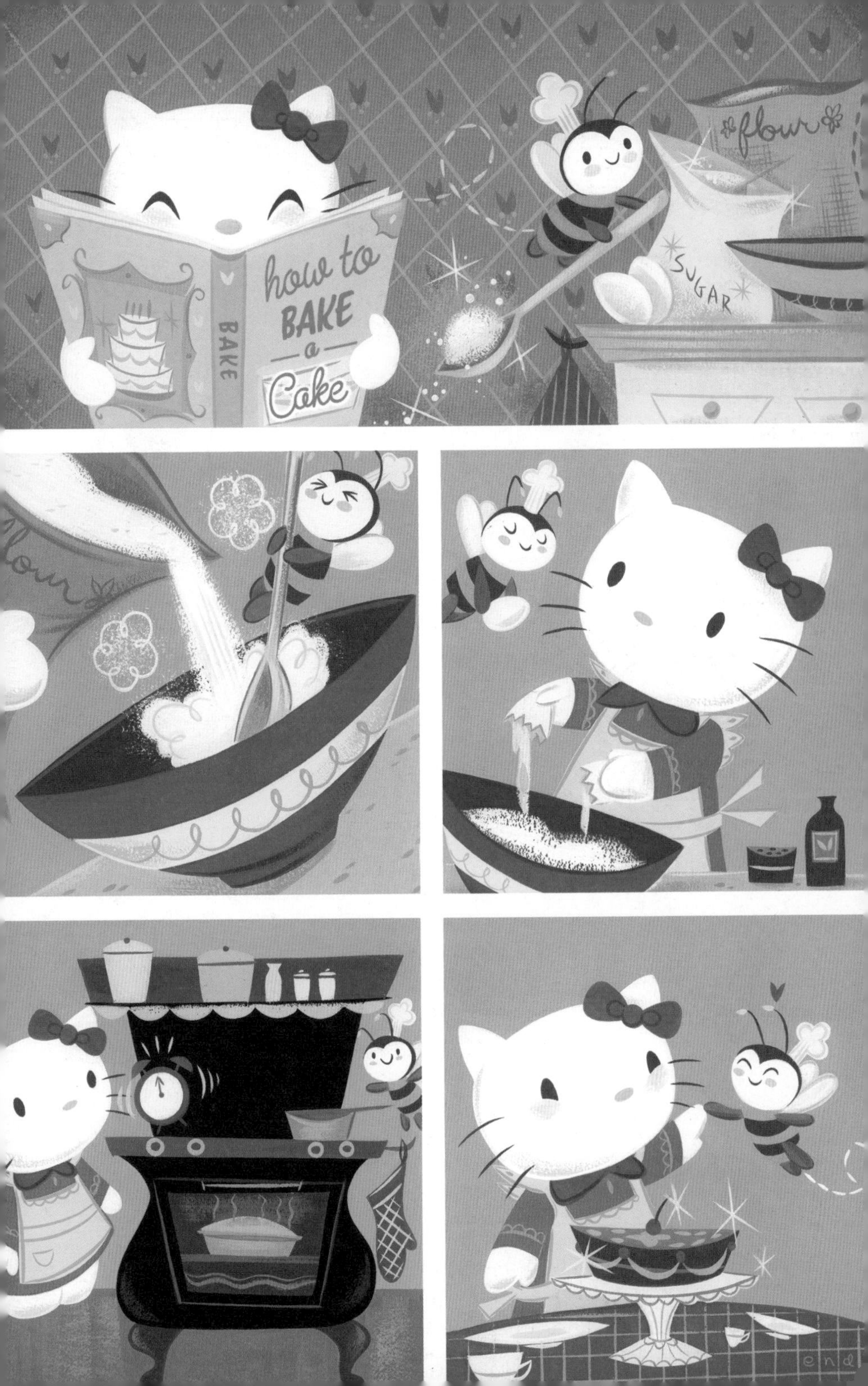
how to
BAKE
a
Cake
BAKE
flour
SUGAR
end

Creators

Jacob Chabot is a New York City-based cartoonist and illustrator. His comics have appeared in publications such as *Nickelodeon Magazine*, *Mad Magazine*, *Spongebob Comics*, and various Marvel titles. He also illustrated *Voltron Force: Shelter from the Storm* and *Voltron Force: True Colors* for VIZ Media. His comic *The Mighty Skullboy Army* is published through Dark Horse and in 2008 was nominated for an Eisner Award for Best Book for Teens.

Jorge Monlongo makes comic books, editorial and children's illustrations and video game designs and paints on canvas and walls. He combines traditional and digital techniques to create worlds in beautiful colors that usually hide terrible secrets. You can see his works in the press (*El Pais*, *Muy interesante*, *Rolling Stone*) and read his comic book series, *Mameshiba*, published by VIZ Media in the USA.

Ian McGinty lives in Savannah, Georgia, and also parts of the universe! Also, Earth. When he isn't drawing comics and rad pictures of octopuses (octopi?), he's laughing at funny-looking dogs and making low-carb burritos! Ian draws stuff for VIZ Media, Top Shelf Productions BOOM! Studios and many more cool folk! But he cannot draw garbage trucks for some reason.

Michael E. Wiggam is a professional comic book colorist whose work includes *Voltron Force* for VIZ Media, *Star Wars: Clone Wars* for Dark Horse Comics, Raymond E. Feist's *Magician Master: Enter the Great One* for Marvel Comics, *R.P.M.* and *I.C.E.* for 12 Gauge Comics, and various other publications. He was born and raised in Florida but has lived in Europe and seven U.S. states. Currently, he is earning an MFA from Savannah College of Art and Design.

Stephanie Buscema is an illustrator and painter from New York. She creates images heavily influenced by music, old monster movies, 1950s' kitsch and vintage children's books. Her days are spent in the studio where she works on cover illustrations, comic art, picture books and paintings for exhibitions.

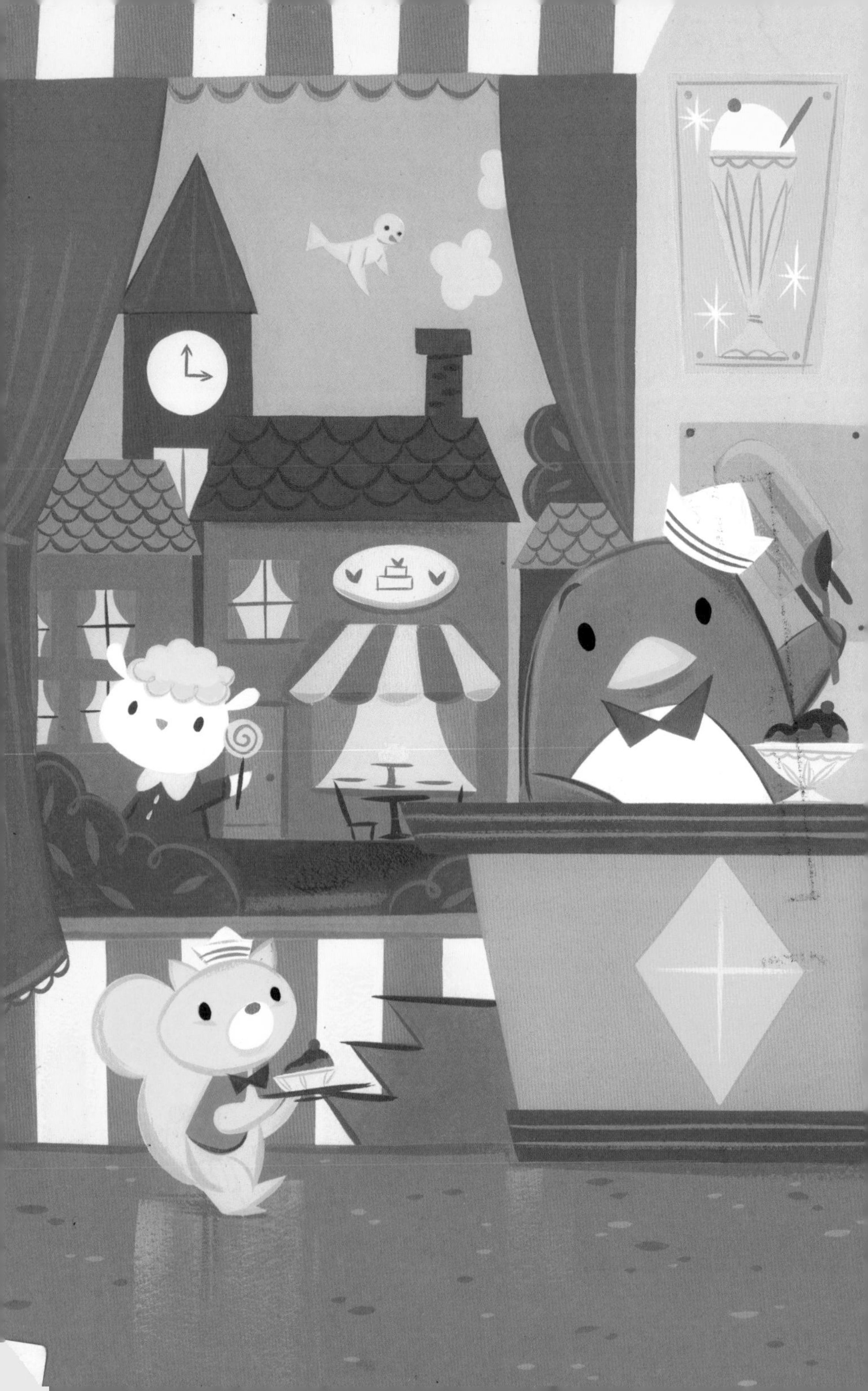